Every Little Thing

Hart's Ridge
Book 12

Kay Bratt

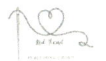

Every Little Thing

A Hart's Ridge Novel

Books by Kay Bratt

<u>Hart's Ridge Series</u>

Hart's Ridge

Lucy in the Sky

In My Life

Borrowed Time

Instant Karma

Nobody Told Me

Hello Goodbye

Starting Over

Blackbird

Hello Little Girl

So This is Christmas

Every Little Thing

<u>By the Sea trilogy</u>

True to Me

No Place too Far

Into the Blue

<u>The Tales of the Scavenger's Daughters series</u>

The Palest Ink

The Scavenger's Daughters

Tangled Vines

Bitter Winds

Red Skies

<u>Life of Willow duology</u>
Somewhere Beautiful
Where I Belong

<u>Standalone Novels</u>
Wish Me Home
Dancing with the Sun
Silent Tears; A Journey of Hope in a Chinese Orphanage
Chasing China; A Daughter's Quest for Truth
A Thread Unbroken
Train to Nowhere
The Bridge
Caroline, Adrift

<u>The Wishing Tree series</u>
The Wishing Tree
Wish You Were Here
Wishful Thinking
A Wish in the Wind

<u>Dragonfly Cove Dog series</u>
Pick of the Litter
Collar Me Crazy

Copyright © 2025 by Kay Bratt

All rights reserved. This book or any portion thereof may not be reproduced or used in any manner whatsoever without the express written permission of the publisher except for the use of brief quotations in a book review.

Printed in the United States of America

First Printing, 2025

Paperback ISBN: 979-8-9918396-2-4

Red Thread Publishing Group

Hartwell, GA 30643

www.kaybratt.com

Cover Design by Elizabeth Mackey Graphic Design

RED THREAD
PUBLISHING GROUP

This book is a fictional dramatization that includes one incident inspired by a real event. Facts to support that incident were drawn from a variety of sources, including published materials and interviews, then altered to fit into the fictional story. Otherwise, this book contains fictionalized scenes, composite and representative characters and dialogue, and time compression, all modified for dramatic and narrative purposes. The views and opinions expressed in the book are those of the fictional characters only and do not necessarily reflect or represent the views and opinions held by individuals on which any of the characters are based.

Chapter One

"*Relax, said the night man, we are programmed to receive. You can check out any time you like, but you can never leave,*" Sam sang softly into Taylor's ear.

She leaned against the railing of their second-floor balcony, his arms around her while they took in the breathtaking view of the resort that sprawled before them. It sat uniquely nestled along a private crescent cove with a swimmable beach—a rarity in the area. The Sea of Cortez stretched out beyond, its waters shimmering in various shades of blue under the sun.

Their room was ocean view, not ocean front, so directly in front of them lay the expansive main pool, its design meandering gracefully with several hidden coves and a thatch-covered bridge crossing one of its detours. The swim-up bar was already buzzing with early patrons ready to party, their laughter mingling with the upbeat music that filled the air. People also lounged on chairs near the pool's edge, while others relaxed in cabanas, their toes peeking out to catch the sun's rays.

Two flights over two thousand miles, plus the stress of the chaotic Los Cabos airport and then the quiet bus ride to the hotel, made her long for an afternoon siesta, but Taylor didn't want to waste what little free time they had. She also wanted to take advantage before homesickness set in and put a shadow over everything. She wondered what Lennon was doing right that instant, and she resisted the urge to check her phone. She didn't want Jo to doubt that Taylor trusted her, so she needed to stick to their planned check ins. Lennon had started scooting over to furniture and attempting to stand, but Jo said she'd try to keep her from taking her first steps until Taylor and Sam returned to see them.

"You're lost in thought," Sam said, his breath warm against her neck, sending a pleasant shiver down her spine. She realized this was their first time alone together in a hotel room, ever. He continued humming the lyrics of the Eagles' famous song, his words more dramatic as he went deeper, sexier, while he swayed with her.

He was really feeling himself and, though she already missed Lennon and Alice and Diesel, she knew Sam needed this respite. They both needed it, to be honest. But Sam also needed some attention in the romantic arena.

"You know," she teased, "it's just a myth that 'Hotel California' is based on a hotel here in Mexico. The Eagles even won a lawsuit against a hotel owner who tried to capitalize on the song's name, forcing them to change it."

"Okay, Miss Google," he chuckled, "but on to more interesting things. Want to get undressed?" He feigned heavy breathing, making her laugh.

"How about what do you want to do first that *doesn't* involve being naked?" she asked. Ever the planner, Taylor appreciated the detailed itinerary the bride and groom had provided for the next few days. Today, however, they were free until the formal welcome dinner that evening. She had purposely left their afternoon open to prove to Sam that she didn't always need a plan.

"You just shot down all my ideas," he joked as he kissed her shoulder. "But I guess we should get in some beach time while we can, then hit the pool to cool off afterward."

She glanced toward the pristine beach to the right of the resort grounds. The scenery was captivating, with the resort's lush gardens blending seamlessly into the sandy shore. The vibrant, sparkling waters of the Sea of Cortez where it met the Pacific Ocean easily lived up to her expectations, the unique blue hues reflecting the depth and beauty of Cabo.

"I'm game," she said. "Let me unpack and put everything away first, then I'll get into my beach clothes." She moved to her suitcase, pleasantly surprised to find it already opened on the bureau. Her dresses hung neatly in the closet, a row of shoes lined up beneath them. The resort's attentive five-star service had taken care of most of the unpacking, allowing her to start their adventure without delay once she rearranged things to her liking.

She felt very self-conscious as they made their way down the stairs and along the walkway to the pool area they'd have to cross or at least go around to get to the beach. She wore a long, white coverup to her ankles, and she strategically carried her straw bag in front of her tummy to hide the bump. Lennon was nine months old, but Taylor couldn't claim she was rocking a beach body in any way. She sure as all get out didn't bring any bikinis with her either.

Three black one-pieces with sufficient covering over her derriere, and three different cover-ups as a secondary curtain. Each outfit would be topped off with a wide-brimmed hat to cover her face and hide her mortification if anyone looked at her too closely.

It was ridiculous how social media kept showing her new

mothers who had slimmed down to their before-baby weight only weeks out. Sometimes a month.

There was nothing normal about that.

Sam said she was gorgeous as they left the room, but he always said that. His job title of husband required it. He looked great, though, in swim trunks she'd grabbed off the clearance rack for him. Fifteen bucks for last year's Nike style was a steal. No one in the wedding party needed to know either.

"Taylor! Sam!" they heard from the pool area.

She looked over the many heads wandering around in the pool to find Cate and Ellis already camped out next to it, looking as though they'd been there all day lounging back in their chairs under a palm tree.

"Want to go talk to them?" Sam asked. "Look at that shirt."

Ellis was wearing a bright yellow shirt with *Cabo, the only place that tequila is cheaper than therapy* written across the front. He waved, urging them to come over.

"Yeah, that's fine," Taylor said, laughing.

She loved it that Ellis never took himself too seriously.

Cate had mentioned they'd be spending most of their water time at the pool, stating that the sun was too brutal at the ocean in the afternoons, so she wasn't surprised they were already there. Ellis didn't use his doctor-knowledge much, but, on the bus ride over, he'd lectured them all sufficiently about the Mexican sun and being very aware of proper sunscreen—especially encouraging those who planned to be doing a lot of drinking, as they were the ones who might forget self-protection in their goal to reach optimum vacation-mode.

"We saved you chairs," Ellis said. "Well, Cate did, as you can tell."

There were at least eight more chairs saved, each with one article of clothing or something from Cate's seemingly bottomless beach bag. A pair of sunglasses on one, a book on another, flip flops separated on two chairs.

Sam laughed. "I think there's plenty of chairs, Cate. The pool police are going to come get you, you keep this up."

Her mom blushed. "I just want to make sure we can all sit together. Have you seen Anna yet?"

"No. On the bus she was just about falling asleep, so I'll bet she's napping," Taylor said, taking the open chaise next to Cate while Sam sat on the one opposite Ellis.

"This is a pretty swanky place, isn't it?" he said, lowering his voice.

"Looks like it, but it's not as costly as you'd think for the wedding," Ellis said. "I think the biggest expense for the guests comes in for flights and wedding wear, on top of the room cost."

That was for sure. Taylor was a bit surprised that Ellis' daughter had put so many stipulations in place for her guests. It was mandatory for them to stay at the same all-inclusive resort that, mind you, didn't allow children. Dress code for the wedding was black-tie. There'd be a five-course reception meal and dancing to follow. Some guests probably even brought something different for the reception wear.

There were other events leading up to the day of the wedding, like the welcome meal that evening, a white party on a boat, tequila-tasting tour, golf, spa day, camel riding, and she couldn't even remember what else.

She and Cate hadn't been included on the bridal party group text that was going back and forth, but Ellis had mentioned some of the details. Taylor hadn't expected her and Sam to be included, but she knew it did hurt Cate's feelings just a little that she wasn't acknowledged as the father-of-the-bride's wife. Not that she wanted to be with them; it was simply about respect and good manners.

"Look over there who is trying to blend in with the kids," Ellis said, slightly nodding toward the pool bar.

Amid many of Madison's friends, as well as the couple themselves, Aunt Heidi was already in the pool, laughing uproariously as she mingled, waving her own personalized thermal cup just over the surface of the water.

Madison's mother had passed years before, so the aunt was standing in as mother-of-the-bride and was taking the role quite possessively. It wouldn't have hurt for Madison to at least invite Cate to participate in the spa day. Cate would've probably politely declined to avoid drama, but the invitation would've been appreciated.

"That's Paul, Heidi's latest boyfriend, standing near the food truck," Ellis added. "Looks like he's not game on joining the party yet. Or she has already gotten mad at him for something. She's always been hard to deal with. Just ask her two ex-husbands."

"I wouldn't want to tangle with her in a dark alley," Sam joked. "She scares me."

"Oh, stop, you two," Cate said softly. "I'm sure she's nice."

Taylor snorted and her mom raised her eyebrows at her, just the barest turn of a grin disappearing off her face as quickly as it had shown, a silent message between them.

They both knew that wasn't true. They'd come face-to-face with dear Aunt Heidi in the main lobby at check in. She'd spoken briefly to Ellis, then pretended not to see Cate as she walked away, her expression like she'd just tasted a turd.

She hadn't acknowledged Taylor either.

Anna had noticed it right away and put on her best airs and went and stood right beside Heidi, towering over the short, dumpy woman and making her look even more like a troll.

Taylor would put Cate against Heidi any day when it came to manners, class, and how they treated others. Heidi wasn't doing herself any favors with her behavior. She was only proving that you could put lipstick on a pig, and it is still a pig.

A huge rush of laughter came from the wedding party in the pool, which was growing quickly. Madison and Brady had joined, too, and their friends were gathered around them.

"They look so happy," Taylor said.

Ellis nodded. "I think so. I know that Brady is a good man and he's just what Madison needs to keep her feet on the ground. He comes from a very modest background and, to see where he is now in his career, and just in life, shows how much grit he has. And he's going to need it to do life with my daughter!"

They all chuckled.

"Ellis, that's not nice," Cate said. "I'm sure she's not that hard to deal with."

"No, that's not what I mean," he said. "Despite the fact that she grew up as a doctor's kid, we didn't live like rich people. Somehow, she got a taste for that lifestyle on her own, after she became an attorney. I fear that sometimes she might follow in my footsteps and place her highest priority on the wrong thing, instead of on family, where it should be."

"In her career, I can see where chasing the next shiny object could become a game no one can win," Sam said.

"It's addictive, for sure," Ellis said, his voice soft and regretful. "I suppose we all have to learn those lessons the hard way."

"Brady seems more family-oriented," Taylor said. "He's really a nice guy. He and his brothers are close too. I could see that just in the small amount of time I saw them interact on the shuttle, and in the lobby. I mean, look at them now. They're always near each other."

When they looked that way again, it was as though Brady heard them. He shot his hand in the air and waved.

"Come get in," he called out. He had a brother on each side

of him and they waved too. Madison looked, then turned her back and faced her aunt.

"Later," Ellis returned, waving back.

"Where is your room?" Taylor asked Cate.

"Building two, third floor. You?"

"Same building, second floor. We have a nice view from our lanai, both the pool and a little bit of the ocean."

"We do too. We must be right on top of each other." She pointed to the end of their building. "Madison and Brady are on that corner. They've got the honeymoon suite with their own private pool."

"Nice," Taylor said, spreading her towel on her chair and getting into a more comfortable position, stretching her long legs the full length. "Oh, wait—do you guys have a concierge? I was taken aback when ours introduced herself and said she was available at any time for anything we need."

Ellis heard them and cut in. "Yes, we have one too. Her name is Rosita."

"That's ours too," Taylor said. "But I'm not going to ask her to do anything, except for maybe make us reservations at the steakhouse. That's the only restaurant that you need to reserve before showing."

"I'll ask her to get my suit ironed," Sam said. "No sense in my struggling when she's paid to make things easier for us."

Taylor blushed. She was always careful when it came to that kind of thing. It embarrassed her to be fussed over. She must've inherited that trait from Cate. Jo was the same, but Lucy and Anna were the opposite.

If Anna's room came with a concierge, and Taylor bet it did, she would probably run her person's legs off. And if Lucy were with them, she'd be having room service with spirits probably every night.

With perfect timing, Madison's best friend, Gia, arrived at

the pool and jumped in with a huge cannonball, causing an uproar of shrieks and laughter.

That was exactly something that Lucy would do too. That's where the similarities stopped though. Gia was a dark-haired Latina siren, her heritage originally Guatemalan but she was as American as apple pie.

Lucy had blonde hair, unless she'd changed it again.

Taylor wondered just where her little sister was now, and when she was coming back. Lucy was always the spice in their gatherings, and she was missed. Johnny was doing fine without her, and didn't ask about her as much now, but she knew deep down that he missed his mom. Taylor had tried to track her, but Lucy was being careful not to leave tracks. She'd come back. She always did.

Chapter Two

The *Lost Highway* wasn't the kind of place you found by accident. It was the kind of place whispered about in dive bar folklore, a secret passed from one drifter to another. Lucy had learned to listen for those whispers.

From the outside, it looked like it had given up on impressing anyone decades ago—a squat, weather-beaten storefront that blended subtly into the rest of the row of shops, located on the backstreet that ran parallel to the historic main downtown. Other than a flickering neon sign that didn't even bother to spell out the whole name. Just *Lost*, you would've never known it was a bar.

Fitting, she thought. That's all she'd been doing—getting lost.

Oklahoma City was a far cry from the small, sleepy towns she'd blown through on her way here. After leaving Georgia, Lucy had zigzagged through the South and Midwest, keeping her movements erratic, never staying anywhere long enough to be noticed.

In Memphis, she'd holed up in a motel on Elvis Presley

Boulevard, the hum of Beale Street a distant echo she didn't have the energy to explore.

In Little Rock, she'd spent four days sleeping in the back of her Jeep in a Walmart parking lot, too paranoid to even check into a motel. The next morning she'd used their ladies' room to cut her long hair into a shoulder-length bob and dyed it a slutty shade of red that would've made Anna go into a conniption. She'd dumped all her artsy-fartsy clothing along the way, trading each item out with things that would match her new lifestyle better, clothes grabbed for a buck or two from thrift shops she stopped at. Like the black leather pants she wore now with the black boots and tank top. An outfit that screamed for people to just look and walk away.

After Little Rock, she'd crossed into Texas, bouncing between Austin and the smaller towns dotting the highway, trying to shake the feeling of being watched. Oklahoma City wasn't the safest bet—too big, too bustling—but it was big enough to disappear in for a while. And Lucy needed a break from the boring backroads.

Inside The Lost Highway, the air was thick with smoke and the heavy scent of spilled beer. This wasn't a bar that pretended to be anything more than what it was. Taxidermy covered the walls—wolves frozen mid-snarl, a bear's head with horns glued onto its skull in some bizarre attempt at humor, and a faded dartboard that had seen more near-misses than hits. The red lacquered booths were cracked and sticky, and a pinball machine in the corner blinked feebly like it was on its last breath. The soundtrack was an erratic mix of old country, grunge, and blues, the volume low enough to let the murmurs of the half-dozen patrons fill the void.

Lucy slid onto a stool at the bar, positioning herself with her back to the wall as always. Her eyes moved methodically across the room, cataloging everyone in sight. A trucker in a camouflage cap sipped his beer at the far end of the bar, his face hidden behind a curtain of smoke. A young couple leaned close at a booth, the woman's laughter a little too loud, the man's eyes darting to the door like he was waiting for someone. By the pinball machine, a kid barely old enough to drink fed quarters into the machine with jittery fingers. None of them looked dangerous. But Lucy had learned the hard way—danger didn't wear a warning sign.

The bartender approached, a woman with purple hair so faded it looked more gray than vibrant. She wiped at the counter with a rag that left smudges instead of cleaning them. "What'll it be?" she asked.

"Maker's. Neat." Lucy's voice was steady, detached. Her face expressionless. She watched as the bartender fumbled with the bottle, her hands trembling slightly. Amateur.

Lucy's attention shifted when the door swung open, letting in a gust of hot air and two newcomers who didn't belong. A woman in a flowy boho dress that screamed Whole Foods shopper and a man in khakis who looked like he'd wandered off a golf course. Lucy tensed instinctively, her fingers curling around the edge of the bar. These were the types who made her skin crawl—not because they were a threat but because they were the opposite. Soft. Oblivious. The kind of people who were friendly and asked too many questions.

The woman's gaze flicked to Lucy, her eyes narrowing on the whiskey in her hand. "What are you drinking?" she asked, her voice cheerful but grating.

"Bourbon," Lucy said flatly.

"What kind?"

"Whatever they gave me." Her tone cut through the woman's forced friendliness like a blade.

The woman recoiled, muttering something under her breath

to the man beside her. Lucy turned back to her drink, her shoulders stiff. People like that didn't understand boundaries. They thought they could just insert themselves into your life, like you owed them something.

After finishing her whiskey, Lucy wandered over to the pool table. A guy in a flannel shirt challenged her to a game, and she let him think he had a chance. She pocketed his five bucks without a hint of remorse, ignoring the way his hand lingered on hers when he handed it over. Disgust coiled in her stomach. She pulled her hand away and wiped it on her black leather pants as she walked back to the bar.

By the time she sank back onto her stool, she was tired of the games. A guy offered to buy her a drink, and she gave him a quick once-over. Dark hair, scruffy beard, the kind of rugged look that might've appealed to her once. She considered it. Maybe he'd be good for a distraction, a night or two of forgetting. But then his phone buzzed, and she caught a glimpse of the screen—a picture of a little girl grinning up at the camera. His daughter, she guessed, from the way his face softened as he answered the call.

No. She wouldn't go there. She hadn't sunk that low. Not yet.

The thought of her son, Johnny, rose unbidden in her mind, and her chest tightened. She missed him with a ferocity that made her hands tremble. But she couldn't go back. Not yet. Not until she was sure the people who were after her had given up.

"Do you sell cigarettes?" she asked the bartender, her voice rasping from the lump in her throat.

The woman shook her head. "There's a gas station next door. You can cut through the back." She gestured to the rear exit.

Lucy nodded and slipped off the stool. Outside, the air was suffocating and dark, thick with a summertime heaviness that sank into your bones. The alley was narrow, lined with dumpsters overflowing with trash. Shadows stretched long and deep, the dim light from the bar's back door barely cutting through the darkness.

She didn't make it far before someone stepped out from the shadows.

"Hey—" she started, but the words were cut off as the person grabbed her, shoving her hard against the wall. Pain exploded in her ribs as she struggled, her breath coming in sharp gasps.

"Let me go, you bastard!" she snarled, thrashing against him, her fingers scrabbling for the knife in her back pocket.

Before she could strike, someone else was there. The guy from the bar—the family man.

"Hey!" he barked, grabbing her attacker and throwing him off. The man hit the ground hard, but the family man didn't stop, landing a solid kick that left the attacker groaning.

Lucy straightened her clothes, her hands shaking as the adrenaline coursed through her. But the punk wasn't done. He grabbed her purse and bolted, disappearing into the shadows before either of them could react.

"Son of a bitch!" Lucy shouted, rage and panic boiling over. Her car keys, her wallet—everything was gone.

The man turned to her, his expression calm but concerned. "You okay?"

"Peachy," she bit out, crossing her arms defensively.

"Come on," he said gently. "Let me give you a ride. Where do you live?"

She hesitated, debating whether to tell him anything. "I don't live around here. Just passing through."

"Then let me get you a motel room," he offered. "You can figure out the rest tomorrow—call your bank, get new keys made."

Every Little Thing

Lucy studied him, her instincts warring with her exhaustion. He seemed ... decent. Maybe even trustworthy.

"Only if you stay with me," she challenged, testing him.

His jaw tightened, but his voice was steady. "I've got a guest room."

For a long moment, neither of them moved, the weight of the night pressing down. Finally, Lucy nodded. "Fine."

She followed him to his truck, the tension between them thick as the Oklahoma summer night. Getting into a vehicle with a stranger was dangerous, she knew that. But, for tonight, danger could just kiss her ass.

———

Lucy woke to the smell of bacon wafting through the air. For a moment, she lay still, the unfamiliar softness of the bed beneath her and the quiet hum of the ceiling fan above making her feel like she was somewhere she didn't belong. Which, of course, she was.

She threw an arm over her eyes and groaned. Last night replayed in disjointed flashes—the bar, the alley, the fight. Him sitting with her on his couch. The way he'd looked at her when she'd practically thrown herself at him, desperate for some kind of distraction. She'd expected him to take her up on it. Most men would have. Instead, he'd handed her a blanket, poured her another drink, and talked to her like she was some wounded stray he'd picked up on the side of the road. And he stayed on his own side of the couch.

A gentleman. Lucy hadn't known what to do with that.

He'd checked on her later, after she'd gotten settled into the guest room and lay staring at the ceiling, unable to sleep.

"You going to be okay?" he said, leaning against the doorframe. He waited for her reply, an agonizingly long minute while she debated speaking.

"Will you just come lay with me?" She finally asked, holding her breath.

He'd crossed the room slowly and kicked off his shoes, then lay on top the comforter beside her, spooning as he pulled her into the curve of his arm. He was fully dressed, but she could still feel his warmth, and his strength.

For the first time in a long time, she felt safe.

She'd fallen asleep quickly after that.

Now she swung her legs over the side of the bed and sat up, scrubbing a hand over her face. On the chair by the window, the robe he'd left for her the night before was neatly folded, a soft gray that looked absurdly comfortable. She grabbed it, slipping it over her tank top and underwear before padding barefoot toward the door.

Coffee. She needed coffee.

Stat.

The kitchen was bright, sunlight streaming through the wide windows that overlooked a backyard bordered with neatly trimmed hedges. The smell of bacon mingled with the rich aroma of brewing coffee, and her stomach growled despite herself.

He was standing barefooted at the stove, spatula in hand, wearing a plain white T-shirt and jeans. He turned when he heard her, his expression unreadable. The scruff he sported for a beard gave him a rumpled, sexy look.

"Morning," he said, his voice low and steady. "Coffee's on the counter. Mugs are in the cabinet above. Flavored creamer in the fridge if you want it."

"Thanks," she muttered, crossing to the counter. She found a mug and poured herself a cup, the heat of it grounding her as she took her first sip. It was strong and black, just the way she liked it. She turned and leaned against the counter, watching him.

"Sleep okay?" he asked, flipping the bacon onto a plate lined with paper towels.

"Fine," she said. She hadn't, really. She'd tossed and turned, her thoughts racing, every creak of the house setting her on edge. But she wasn't about to admit that.

"Good." He set the plate on the table, gesturing for her to sit. "Eggs will be ready in a minute. Help yourself."

Lucy hesitated, then slid into one of the chairs. The table was small but solid, the kind of furniture that spoke of quiet, steady living. The walls of the kitchen were adorned with framed prints—decent art, she noted. Not cheap stuff from a department store. The place was tidy, too, everything in its place.

"Nice house," she said, glancing around.

"Thanks. Belonged to my parents. I've been fixing it up a little at a time."

She nodded, filing that piece of information away.

"You never told me your name," he said. "I told you mine."

Damned if she could remember what his was…

"In case you forgot, I'm Graham."

She thought fast. "Lily."

"There you go," he teased. "Now was that so hard? Last night you acted like I was CIA or something when I asked."

She felt a flash of panic. Was that a hint? Was he someone to worry about?

Now she couldn't remember his story. What did he do for a living? Where was the kid she'd seen on his phone?

He joined her at the table a few minutes later, setting a plate of scrambled eggs and toast in front of her. She eyed it suspiciously, but the smell was too tempting to resist. She took a bite, and it was good. Too good. It made her stomach twist with something uncomfortably close to gratitude.

"Here," he said, sliding a piece of paper and his phone across the table toward her. "That's the number to a local shop that does towing and keys. They'll get your Jeep here and make you a new set of keys for less than what a dealership would charge. You probably need to call your bank or something too. Shut down any credit cards you have. Get them reissued."

She'd left those at home. Too easy to track. Most of her cash was hidden in her jeep, but the thief had gotten her identification and a hundred bucks. And the keys. She stared at the paper, her fingers brushing the edge of it. "Why are you helping me?" she asked, her voice sharper than she intended.

He shrugged. "It's not a big deal. You needed help. Pretty simple."

She snorted. "Nothing's that simple."

"Maybe not. But it doesn't have to be complicated either." He leaned back in his chair, studying her. "You're welcome to stay a day or two, if you need to. Give you some time to figure things out."

She'd spent so long running, so long looking over her shoulder, that the idea of staying anywhere—even for a couple of days—felt foreign. But as she looked around the kitchen, her eyes lingering on the clean lines of the table, the art on the walls, and the light streaming in through the windows, she couldn't help but think that maybe ... maybe it wouldn't be the worst place to hide out for a little while.

"I'll think about it," she said finally, her tone cautious.

He nodded, as if he'd expected that. "Fair enough."

They ate in silence after that, the only sound the soft clink of forks against plates. Lucy's mind raced, already spinning stories she might feed him if he pressed her for details. Last night, she'd given him some half-baked lie about being on the road for work, and he'd bought it. Or at least he'd pretended well. Pity softened people up, she'd learned that a long time ago. And he seemed like the kind of guy who wanted to help. She'd use that for as long as she needed to, and then she'd be gone. Like always.

But, for now, she'd take the bacon and the coffee. And maybe ... maybe a little bit of rest.

Chapter Three

Taylor took Sam's hand for support and boarded the gorgeous, chartered boat for the white party and reminded herself to just smile and pretend she wasn't sweating down to the deepest depths of her soul. She was grateful for her last-minute decision to ditch the fancy white pants and blouse for a short dress with vibrant flowers along the hem. It may have technically violated the all-white dress code, but the oppressive heat would've made anything else unbearable for day three in the relentless Mexico heat.

She officially knew what it really meant when someone said they felt like they were melting. All she could think about was a cool shower and cranking the air conditioning up in their room until icicles hung from her nose.

Madison looked ever the perfectly-styled bride wearing a super short white dress, a sash that read *bride* across her chest, and four-inch spiked heels that Taylor was surprised the captain allowed on the boat. Her best friend and maid of honor, Gia, was by her side as usual, flashing a smile at everyone and doing any and everything that Madison asked of her.

Guests milled about the deck, their white outfits catching

the fading sunlight, though some already sported the flushed look of too many pre-party tequila shots. The music blared, a rhythmic thumping that seemed to compete with the crash of the waves against the boat. The sea was unusually rough, and Taylor grabbed the railing as the vessel rocked sharply to one side.

A group of young women shrieked as their drinks splashed over the rims of their glasses.

"Wow, this is worse than I expected," Taylor muttered, clutching her straw bag tightly. Sam, steady on his feet despite the boat's erratic movements, placed a hand on her back.

"You okay?" he asked.

She didn't want to give Madison more fodder to dislike her family, so she gave him a brave thumbs up and smiled. "Yeah, just trying not to fall overboard." She laughed nervously, watching a particularly strong wave make a waiter stagger sideways, the tray of shots he carried tilting precariously. Somehow, he didn't spill a drink, an impressive feat for sure.

Ellis' voice carried over the din as he and Cate joined them under the shade. "Looks like we're in for a wild ride. Big crowd but I didn't see Heidi come on board."

Sam smirked. "She's not here. I saw Paul practically dragging her out of the pool and back toward their room earlier. She could barely stand. Guess she started the party a little too early."

Ellis frowned. "That's too bad. I think this was supposed to be the highlight of all the events leading up to tomorrow. Not a good look either. I can't say much, though, considering that Patrick didn't even make it to Mexico."

Cate gave his arm a squeeze. Patrick was Ellis' son, and there'd been some drama between him and his sister, though Ellis didn't say exactly what. It must've been deep considering he wouldn't even attend her wedding.

Nearby, Madison's grandmother sat on a couch under the shade of the top platform, wearing her Sunday best and a stoic expression, her white skirt fluttering in the wind. She gave Taylor a tight smile as their eyes met, and Taylor returned it. They appeared to be the only two nondrinkers on the boat.

As the boat lurched again, Taylor's attention was drawn to one more—a pregnant young woman perched at a high table near the edge of the boat, clutching a can of ginger ale. Her pale and shiny face contrasted sharply with her dark hair, and she gripped the railing so tightly her knuckles were white.

Taylor's stomach turned just watching her sway with the motion of the boat.

Suddenly, the girl stumbled toward the stairs leading below deck, her hand covering her mouth. Taylor didn't hesitate. "I'll be right back," she told Sam, already following the young woman.

She found her in the small bathroom, hunched over the toilet, retching violently. Taylor quickly gathered the girl's long hair and held it back, murmuring soothing words as she gently rubbed her back.

When the girl paused, Taylor got paper towels, wet a stack, and brought them over.

"Here, you can wash your face," she said. "We can go up when you're ready. Don't try to rush it."

The girl, whose name Taylor hadn't caught, gasped between heaves, blotting her face. "I thought I could handle this," she croaked. "But the rocking ... and the heat ..."

"Shh, it's fine," Taylor reassured her. "Happens to the best of us. I saw quite a few green faces up top.""

A moment later, Cate appeared, an ice pack in hand. "I thought you might need this," she said, her calm presence instantly soothing.

"Thank you," Taylor said, taking the ice pack and gently pressing it against the back of the girl's neck. "This will help."

The girl's breathing began to steady, and she leaned back against the wall, her face glistening with sweat. "I'm sorry," she mumbled. "I should've stayed behind, but Madison begged me to come."

"Don't be sorry," Cate said firmly. "The important thing is you're okay. What's your name, sweetheart?"

"Emma," the girl replied weakly.

"Well, Emma, you're a good friend, but let's get you back upstairs for some fresh air," Cate said, helping her to her feet. Taylor kept a steadying hand on Emma's arm as they navigated the narrow winding staircase back to the deck.

The scene above was no less chaotic. Guests clung to anything solid as the boat continued to pitch and roll. The music thumped on, oblivious to the discomfort of some of its audience.

Taylor guided Emma to a quieter corner near the railing, away from the crowd.

"Here," Cate said, handing Emma a bottle of water. "Sip this slowly."

Emma nodded gratefully, her color beginning to return. "Thank you. Both of you. My husband is here somewhere. He told me he wouldn't drink since I can't, but the guys talked him into it. He's no help at all."

"Yikes, he's in trouble later," Taylor said with a smile. "Just take it easy. He'll find you soon. The party can survive without us for a little while."

Emma laughed weakly. "Yeah, but I'm not sure I'll survive the party."

Taylor glanced toward the crowd, where laughter and clinking glasses filled the air despite the boat's relentless rocking. They were gathering at the bow of the boat, arranging themselves around Madison and Brady for photos.

Madison was waving at her dad to come join, but, again, she noticed that no one paid any mind to Cate. She sat looking poised and classy, sipping her drink as she pretended not to care that she wasn't included.

Taylor leaned against the railing, the cool breeze a welcome relief against her flushed skin. She wouldn't say it to anyone but Sam, but she would be glad when the week was over, and she could get back to her life. Back to Lennon, Alice, Diesel and all the animals. The comfort and safe feeling of her house and the farm. And hopefully ... maybe even her job. She planned to talk to Sam about that before they left Mexico. The sheriff was still waiting on an answer.

He would have to wait though. In the meantime, she was learning that vacations weren't ever going to be her thing. She liked routine and familiar things. Mexico made her nervous. Being away from home too. It felt unnatural.

Not so for Anna. In the last few days, she'd somehow become the focus of a young man at least fifteen years her junior. One of Brady's best friends from childhood, and they called him Hazard. He was a tall, lanky fellow, and maybe not the most attractive of the bunch of millennials, but surely the most interesting.

Hazard was loud and hilarious, and danced like a crazy scarecrow, but he made Anna laugh and feel young, and she looked like she was having such a great time that Taylor couldn't help but be happy for her. Even now, somehow Anna had made it into the wedding party photo, standing in the shadow of Hazard's arm around her shoulders while he chose to look at her instead of the photographer. There was no doubt that even if they hadn't already, the week wasn't going to end without the two of them coming together behind closed doors.

Good for Anna. She needed the attention after all she'd been through with her piece of crap ex, Pete. Anna juggled a lot too. Work at Gray's Escape, nursing school, her kids.

When they got back, it would soon be time for her graduation. She'd successfully flown through the accelerated nursing program with top grades. She'd excelled at her clinicals too. All that was left was for her to take her national exam. By October she would hopefully be a licensed nurse practitioner for the state of Georgia. They were all so proud of her and the way she'd taken control of her life and future.

A rogue wave hit, and the boat rocked violently, bringing out a shriek in chorus as everyone grabbed for someone or something to hang onto.

"My God, when is this going to end?" Taylor said under her breath. Even the grandmother was starting to look a bit green and irritated. Not the rest of them though. The younger of the crowd were too far gone on tequila shots to care about a bit of rocking and rolling.

Taylor had never seen so much partying in her life than she had in the last three days. After the sit-down welcome dinner the first night, the wedding party had shut the resort bar down before gathering on the patio with Madison and Brady and drinking until it was time for the sun to come up and they'd gone down to the beach to watch the sunrise. A tequila sunrise, they'd said the next morning when the guys had gathered, hung over but at least on time, to meet to go play golf and the gals to head off to the spa.

Same thing the next day except it was tequila tours and camel riding. After that, they'd met at the pool, hanging out at the swim-up bar drinking until dinner, when everyone broke up to get ready and meet, then off to the resort bar for the rest of the evening.

Cate had heard about it from Ellis, and she was keeping Taylor informed.

She stood next to her now, her eyes scanning the people cheesing for the photos before settling on Emma again. "You're good at this, you know," she said softly to Taylor.

Taylor tilted her head. "At what?"

"Taking care of people. I'm super proud of you, Taylor. Of who you are."

Taylor blushed, her gaze drifting to Emma, who was now leaning her head back and breathing deeply, keeping her eyes on the solid line of the horizon. Hopefully she'd be okay until they made it back.

The words her mother said echoed in Taylor's mind, filling her with something warm. No matter how stable and successful you think your life is—or how independent you think you are—there always seemed to be an unquenchable thirst for your parents' approval. It had taken half her lifetime to find it too.

"Maybe. But it helps to have a good team. You're a great wingman, Mom."

Chapter Four

The world had a way of dressing up for love, Taylor thought as she took in the light-strewn lanai shimmering in the late afternoon sunlight. The wedding guests gathered there, at the very edge of the resort where the sound of waves crashing against the shore mingled with soft classical music from a live string quartet.

Taylor adjusted the hem of her flowing navy gown as she stood to the side and waited for Sam. He'd forgotten his pocket square and ran back to the room, saying he needed it to mop his brow. The tranquil setting was stunning for a ceremony, yet the heat was nearly unbearable. She discreetly wiped sweat from her brow with her fingertips, wishing the breeze from the ocean would pick up just a little.

The aisle was lined with ivory rose petals, and lanterns hung from the beams of the lanai, their soft light twinkling against the deepening blue of the late afternoon sky. Guests murmured quietly as they waited, fanning themselves with programs that doubled as makeshift shields against last rays of the sun going down.

Sam returned to Taylor's side, offering his arm. "Ready?" he asked with a reassuring smile. He knew she felt out of her element, all fancied up in a dress and heels. However, he looked so dashing in his tux. She hoped they could get someone to take a photo of them later before they got too frazzled from the heat.

"Ready as I'm gonna get," she said, slipping her arm into his. Together, they walked down the aisle and found their seats.

Cate turned and smiled at Taylor from her seat on the front row, her eyes already glistening with tears. Taylor gave her a quick wink before taking her seat and turning her attention toward the couples waiting to come down the aisle arm-in-arm.

Anna arrived on Hazard's arm, and he let her slide in, then he joined the others waiting to walk the bridesmaids in.

It had started.

"Look, that has to be Ellis' son," Anna whispered. "He must've just arrived."

Taylor nodded. The young man looked exactly like his dad, except slimmer and younger. He was extremely tan, and she remembered that Ellis said he lived on Maui and was a big surfer and a champion spearfisherman. She was glad he'd made it after all.

Once everyone in the wedding party was seated, the music paused and then the wedding march began. Everyone turned, anxious to see the bride, but first a chuckle ran through the aisles when it was Grandmother first, scattering more flower petals from a basket she carried as she made her way to her seat near Cate.

Finally, Madison stood at the entrance of the lanai, radiant in her long, flowing gown. Her auburn hair was styled with part of it swept up, the rest cascading in elegant ringlets down her back. Her makeup was flawless, her cheeks glowing as if lit from within. Taylor's breath caught, for Madison looked absolutely beautiful.

Brady, standing at the altar in his sharp black tuxedo, visibly choked up as soon as he saw his bride. His eyes filled with tears, and he hastily swiped at them with the back of his hand, prompting an audible "aww" from the crowd.

Ellis appeared at Madison's side, his face beaming with pride and emotion. He held his daughter's arm tightly, his steps steady but deliberate as they made their way down the aisle.

Taylor's heart ached as she saw Cate silently crying, her emotions clearly stirred by the bittersweet scene. Cate knew how deeply Ellis loved his children and how much it had hurt him when they initially resisted his relationship with her. And, now, here he was, beaming with pride, walking his daughter toward her future while his son, unexpectedly present, stood waiting at the front, his presence a subtle seal of approval for the union.

The ceremony was being held under the lanai's canopy, with the ocean stretching endlessly behind the officiant. Just as the vows began, a group of original Mexican cowboys rode horses across the beach in the distance, their silhouettes striking against the golden sands and the vibrant blue waves. The guests murmured in admiration, the scene looking like something out of a romantic movie.

The officiant smiled warmly as he began the ceremony. "Madison and Brady, today is the day you've chosen to start your lives together as husband and wife. Please remember that marriage is built on love, trust, and, as I've learned in my years of officiating weddings, a good sense of humor." The guests chuckled lightly, the mood shifting to one of ease.

Madison and Brady exchanged vows, their voices trembling with emotion. When it was Brady's turn, he paused, his face breaking into a grin. "Madison, I promise to love you, to cherish you, and to always ..." He paused dramatically. "To always let you choose the Netflix series we're going to binge, even if I'd rather watch sports."

The guests burst into laughter, and Madison covered her mouth with her hand, chuckling through her tears. "And I promise," she said in response, "to always support you, even if it means cheering for fantasy football ... again."

The giggles rippled through the lanai, breaking the tension of the heat and emotion. Ellis visibly wiped his eyes as he stood at the altar, watching his daughter and son-in-law exchange their promises. For a moment, his gaze shifted to his son, who caught his eye and gave him a small nod. Taylor saw Ellis' throat tighten, his pride and love for both his children written all over his face.

Finally, the officiant declared, "You may now kiss the bride."

Brady didn't hesitate. He swept Madison into his arms and kissed her deeply, their love evident in the way they clung to each other. As the guests erupted into applause, he dipped her dramatically, earning whistles and cheers from the crowd. The moment was pure magic, the perfect culmination of a heartfelt and joyous ceremony.

Taylor clapped along with the rest of the guests, her heart full as she watched Madison and Brady coming up the aisle, hand in hand, their smiles lighting up the night.

It was nearly seven in the evening when Taylor and Sam stepped onto the Sky Bar terrace, and were met with a beautiful sight of black, white, and gold touches all around. Tables were set for dinner on white cloths, multiple glasses and cutlery at each setting, elaborate floral arrangements peppered throughout.

Taylor was glad to be able to sit and get off her feet for a bit. After the ceremony, they'd all stood around for cocktails, waiting to be called up to the reception.

Now the golden hour bathed the space in a warm, amber glow, reflecting off the ocean waves below and the coastline stretching endlessly to the side. The terrace was quickly alive with chatter and laughter as guests began to mingle, most still wearing their formalwear, and a few who had gone to their rooms and changed into something else dressy, but less formal.

Taylor's gaze swept over the meticulously arranged tables, taking in the name cards glittering in the light, everything planned down to the last detail, including where they'd sit.

"Look at that," Sam said, nodding toward the entrance where a wall of shot glasses greeted the guests. Each one bore the embossed initial of the wedding couple's last name, a tiny keepsake from the wedding. "Madison and Brady really outdid themselves."

Taylor chuckled, adjusting the strap of her emerald-green dress. "But a shot glass wall? I hope the bartenders are ready for another long night."

They moved toward their assigned table, where Cate and Ellis were already seated, joined by Anna and Brady's brothers.

Her sister, of course, was dressed in a spectacular off-the-shoulder ivory gown, sequins sparkling under the light. She was in her element, loving having been invited to such a swanky event. She had picked out Taylor's dress too. A much more understated dress, dark green with tulle, or something like that. No high heels for her though. An inch or so was still enough to make her feet swell immediately in the humid Mexican air.

Ellis stood to pull out a chair for Taylor. "You two clean up well," he said with a warm smile.

"Not too shabby yourself," Sam quipped, clapping Ellis on the back as they all settled in. He turned to her mother. "Cate, you look gorgeous."

Cate blushed and thanked him. Anna had helped their mom pick her dress too. A very classy off-the-shoulder black floor-length gown. It was listed online under the mother-of-the-bride section, not that Cate was trying to rally for the title, but she wanted Ellis to be proud of how she looked. Proud to have her on his arm, even though she didn't feel worthy of it, she'd confided to Taylor.

Anna had done Cate's hair. She and Taylor bit back what they really wanted to say when Heidi was talking about all the women in the wedding party meeting in Madison's room for hair and makeup, loud enough to let them know that Cate was not invited.

Now, Cate looked better than any of the women her age at the event. Her hair in a French twist, diamond-encrusted bobby pins catching the lights when she moved her head. She'd done her own makeup, applying it so subtle it almost appeared she didn't wear any, but so perfect it set her eyes off.

It was obvious that Ellis couldn't take his eyes off her. But then, it was always that way. Theirs was a true love—no frills needed.

"Did Jo call you about a dog named Louise?" Cate asked, leaning close to Taylor.

"No. What is it?"

"A little four-pound Papillon mix was abandoned at the vet with multiple broken bones. Hip, pelvis and both legs. Dr. Terry said she looks like she's been drop-kicked because there aren't any external injuries. She's a young one too."

Cate took her phone out and showed Taylor a photo of a blenheim-colored tiny dog, her ears straight up like they were gathering information. She had the softest brown eyes and sweetest expression. The dog was laid on her side, her back legs lying limply beneath her.

Taylor shook her head in disgust. She wished she could get her hands on the piece of shit who thought they were so tough, picking on a defenseless animal.

"Do they have a name for who left her?" she asked.

"Afraid not," Cate said, shaking her head.

"What do we need to do next?"

"Jo is already on it. She told Dr. Terry we would take financial responsibility and guardianship. Animal Control is going to waive the ten-day wait period, and Louise will get surgery on one side later today. If it goes well and she recovers on that side, they'll address the other side or possibly amputate the other leg. This is going to be pricey though. At least five grand for the first surgery alone, but I agreed to go ahead with it. We'll have to find the donations somewhere."

"Agree, 100%," Taylor said. How could they say no? Every life has value and, if they could save the little thing, that's what the rescue was for. Sissy would've approved.

"Jo already has a medical foster in mind. Pat Key with Homeward Bound has agreed to take her home when she's ready."

"Oh, that's great. Pat is the best."

"And I forgot to tell you," Cate said, "Jo has agreed to help the theatre group again. She's going to be working with the costume designer. Just from home. She's not ready to go back there, she said, but she's dipping her toe in this way. I'm so relieved that she's finally going to do something that brings her joy."

They all nodded. Jo had been through a lot. It was about time she started to come out of her shell a bit. But now Taylor felt even worse for leaving her holding all the responsibilities of managing the farm and the kids.

The white-gloved server drew her attention and, as the first course was served—a delicate ceviche paired with crisp white wine—the conversation turned to less dramatic things at home. Taylor glanced at the flickering candlelight, her mind drifting.

"Jo's got her hands full," she said, swirling her wine absentmindedly. "Lennon, Alice, Johnny ... costumes and now this little dog, Louise. I hope she's holding up okay."

"I'm sure she's got it under control," Sam reassured her, placing a hand over hers. "We'll be back soon enough. Just try to enjoy this, Tay. You've earned it."

Cate leaned in, her voice soft. "And Lucy? Have you heard from her?

Taylor's expression faltered. "Nothing. No contact now for five months. But Sam's right—this is not unusual for her. She'll come home when she's ready."

Cate nodded thoughtfully. "At least Quig's doing well. Moving into Lucy's cabin temporarily was a blessing for her. A safe place for her kids to visit. I like that she's really becoming part of the family team. It's giving her the confidence she needs not to fall back into bad habits."

"I agree. And when Lucy comes home, we might just have to talk about building one more cabin. Quig could eventually pay rent, if we do. Having an extra set of hands at the farm permanently would be great."

As the courses progressed—a perfectly seared fish with vibrant sides—the mood lightened. When dessert arrived, the speeches began. Ellis rose first, raising his glass. "Madison," he began, his deep voice carrying across the terrace, "your mom would be so proud of the woman you've become. She's here tonight, in spirit, watching over you and Brady. I know she's smiling."

Taylor glanced at Cate and noticed a shimmer of tears in her mother's eyes. Cate caught her looking and smiled, dabbing at her cheek.

Madison's Aunt Heidi followed, swaying slightly as she stood. Her speech began with the words, "When you know, you know, you know ..." she rambled, barely making sense as everyone nodded awkwardly until she finally took her seat again.

Cate would've done a better job, Taylor thought to herself.

As dessert plates were cleared, the clinking of a fork against a glass silenced the room. All eyes turned to Madison's grandmother as she rose from her seat, her hands trembling slightly as she adjusted the microphone. Her voice, though frail, carried warmth that immediately commanded attention. She looked regal, her silver hair pinned neatly and a posture that spoke of dignity and grace.

"Tonight, as we celebrate Madison and Brady," she began, her gaze sweeping the room, "I can't help but reflect on a day just like this one, so many years ago. On this very date, I married my Henry." A collective murmur rippled through the crowd. The revelation added an unexpected layer of sentiment to the evening.

"Henry and I," she continued, her voice softening, "were just two kids from a small town, with big dreams and empty pockets. Our wedding wasn't held in a place as grand as this, but in a modest church with peeling paint and creaky pews. Instead of a five-course meal, our reception menu was made up of potluck dishes brought by neighbors. Cakes and cookies baked with good wishes. And instead of shot glasses, our favors for our guests were little handwritten notes, thanking everyone for their love and support."

A tear slipped down her cheek, but her smile never wavered. "Yet, despite its simplicity, it was the most magical day of my life. I've never once thought of how modest my wedding was or wished it had been bigger." She waved her hand around the room. "I'm so glad my granddaughter is able to have the day of her dreams, but, for me, I didn't need all this because we were celebrating a special kind of love—a love that carried us through hardships, joys, and everything in between for fifty-seven beautiful years."

The room was captivated, hanging on her every word, now. Tears ready to pounce. "Henry would have loved to be here tonight. He always had a way of lighting up a room, much like Madison does. And I have no doubt he's smiling down on all of us right now, especially you, my darling." She turned her gaze to Madison, her eyes shimmering with pride and love.

"So, as you begin this journey, my wish for you both is that you hold on to each other tightly. Through the laughter, through the tears, through the mundane and the extraordinary. Because, in the end, it's not the grand gestures or the big milestones that make a marriage. It's not about putting on a show or about the expensive trips or fancy jewelry. It's the small, everyday acts of love that build a life together."

By the time she finished, there wasn't a dry eye in the room. The applause that followed was thunderous, with many guests standing to honor her heartfelt words.

Madison dabbed at her tears, leaning into Brady as her grandmother sat back down, her face radiant with satisfaction.

Next came the best man, Brady's younger brother, Nathan. A sharp contrast to the emotional moment just passed, Nathan's mischievous grin and relaxed posture hinted that he was about to lighten the mood.

"Well," Nathan began, clearing his throat dramatically, "I guess I've got a tough act to follow. Thanks for that, Grandmother." The room erupted in laughter, a much-needed release of emotion. He leaned into the mic, his tone playful. "You know, when Brady first told me he was getting married, I wasn't sure I believed him. I mean, this is the same guy who used to live off instant ramen and thought a fitted sheet was just a fancy blanket." More laughter echoed through the venue, with Brady shaking his head and grinning at Nathan.

"My brothers and I had only each other, and Brady did a fine job of keeping us in line and has done well making a life for himself. But he still didn't know caviar from a cocktail weenie until Madison came along," Nathan continued, his tone softening just a touch, "and suddenly my brother was ... well, different. Better. Cleaner, for one thing. The guy actually started ironing his pants and eating vegetables. And I'll be damned if he doesn't match his socks to his shirts now. And if that's not true love, I don't know what is."

The crowd roared, with even the bride laughing so hard she wiped tears from her eyes.

"But in all seriousness," Nathan said, his expression growing sincere, "Brady's come a long way from the guy who used to duct-tape his car together. And that's thanks to you, Madison. You've brought out the best in him, and I can't think of anyone more perfect to be his partner in this crazy thing we call life." He raised his glass. "So, here's to Madison and Brady. May your love be as enduring as Grandmother's stories, as strong as duct tape, and as sweet as this cake we're about to eat. Cheers!"

The room erupted in applause and laughter, the perfect mix of heartfelt and humorous. As Nathan stepped away from the mic, Brady pulled him into a brotherly hug, clearly touched despite the teasing. The speeches had set the tone for the night —a blend of nostalgia, love, and lighthearted fun—and, as the music started up again, the guests hit the dance floor with renewed energy, ready to celebrate the new chapter in Madison and Brady's lives.

As the formalities ended, Madison and Brady disappeared for a quick change. When they returned, Madison wore a short, white sequined dress and high heels, both made for dancing. The crowd erupted into cheers as the couple performed a choreographed routine. Taylor even saw Brady's lips moving to count under his breath as he did his best to follow the steps.

The theatrical lift at the end drew gasps, followed by a dramatic dip that had everyone clapping and whistling.

Brady's brothers rushed the dance floor and gave him high-fives, and soon most of the wedding party was out there, too, including Hazard and Anna. As the tequila continued to be poured, the guys came out of their jackets and even some of them down to bare chests.

Sam kept his shirt on but proved he could keep up and cut a rug with the guys. He took Cate out for a spin when Taylor's feet began to ache after a few dances. She excused herself and wandered to the edge of the terrace, letting the ocean breeze cool her flushed cheeks.

The rhythmic crash of the waves below was soothing. She watched as a young couple from the wedding party, clearly intoxicated, ventured toward the beach. A security guard across the way noticed them, too, his walkie-talkie crackling as he descended to bring them back.

"It's not safe out there at night," she overheard the security guard say loudly, scolding them as he escorted them back up.

She wondered what was so dangerous. The surf? The locals?

As far as she could tell, the resort felt very secure. The staff were everywhere, walkie-talkies on their hips and purpose in their steps. You couldn't even park at the hotel or walk in unless the security guard found your name on the list of incoming guests. Uber drivers had to wait outside the gates. She had to give it to the management, security seemed on point.

Strong arms wrapped around her from behind and she felt the familiar pull of Sam's lips brushing against her ear. "Your mom sent me over here to check on you. What's got you so serious?" he murmured, his voice low and warm.

Taylor leaned into him, closing her eyes. "Just thinking how nice this is. Being here, with you. It's been a long road, hasn't it?"

"It has," Sam said, holding her tighter. "But we're here now. That's all that matters."

"When you know, you know," she said, and they both laughed.

"Oh Lord ... that woman should've stayed off the sauce," Sam said. "I don't know what the hell she was trying to say."

Their laughter trailed off and left Taylor with a smile. She felt the tension ease from her shoulders. Tomorrow, she thought. Once this day was over and behind them, she'd talk to him about going back to work. For now, she wanted to savor the moment, the breeze, the distant hum of laughter and music—the life of peace and good health that they were finally reclaiming.

Chapter Five

Some mornings never ask if you're ready, they just arrive with a bang. A loud pounding on the hotel door jolted Taylor and Sam out of the last blissful bits of slumber, jarring them fully awake. Taylor stumbled out of bed, throwing on her robe, and opened the door to find Brady standing there. His tuxedo shirt from the previous night was rumpled, his hair disheveled, and his face pale with panic.

"Madison's missing," he blurted out, his voice trembling. "I can't find her anywhere."

Taylor's irritation evaporated instantly. "What do you mean she's missing?"

"The last time I saw her was late last night. She was sitting by our room's private pool with Gia and a few others, drinking. One by one, everyone left except Gia. I went to take a shower, thinking she'd get the hint. Madison said she'd come in after Gia left, but, when I got out of the shower, they were still out there. I took another shot, lay down on the bed, and must've passed out. When I woke a little bit ago, they were both gone."

"Early morning yoga maybe? Walk on the beach?" Taylor asked.

"I'm telling you, she never came to bed last night. I know she didn't."

Her stomach sank.

Sam called out. "Have you checked Gia's room?"

Brady nodded frantically. "Yes, but no one answered. I've been to the front desk, but they said they haven't seen her."

Taylor placed a steadying hand on his arm. "Okay, Brady. We'll figure this out. Just take a deep breath. Let's call Ellis first and see if he's seen her."

Sam was already up, pulling on a shirt as Taylor grabbed her phone and dialed Ellis. The call connected quickly, and Ellis answered, his voice groggy but alert when he heard the urgency in Taylor's tone.

"No, I haven't seen her," Ellis said. "Cate and I will be right over."

Minutes later, Ellis and Cate arrived, concern all over their faces.

"Brady, do you and Madison share locations on your phones?" Taylor asked.

He looked sick at his stomach as he pulled a phone from his pocket. "This is her phone. She left it."

That wasn't good. Taylor quickly laid out a plan, trying to keep her own growing worry hidden. "Brady—wake up the bridesmaids and ask each one if they've seen Madison or Gia. Sam and Ellis, go to the pool bar and talk to any guests you see. Then get a few people together to check the beach; maybe they went to see the sunrise and fell asleep. Oh, see if Heidi has seen her."

Ellis nodded, already moving. "We're on it."

"Cate, let me get dressed and then we'll go together," Taylor continued. "We need to get the manager to let us into Gia's room."

After she threw on some clothes, they made their way to the front desk.

Taylor and Cate walked briskly across the cool marble floors of the resort lobby, their sandals tapping against the polished surface. The early morning air felt thick, the humidity already heavy, promising to be a brutally hot day.

The resort was beginning to stir, a few early risers sipping coffee near the massive floor-to-ceiling windows, oblivious to the growing panic seething beneath Taylor's skin.

Taylor and Cate headed straight for the front desk, cutting through the sleepy resort atmosphere with a sharp urgency that made them stand out.

Rafael, the resort manager, was leaning against the counter, speaking to a staff member in hushed Spanish. His demeanor was smooth and controlled, his authority obvious.

Taylor went to him and didn't wait for pleasantries. "We need access to Gia Castillo's room right now. It's an emergency."

Rafael sighed, rubbing his temple as if this were nothing more than an inconvenience. "Señora, we have policies in place to protect our guests' privacy. As I said to the groom earlier this morning, our security team is looking, and I do not think—"

Cate, standing beside Taylor in her linen blouse and slacks, lifted her chin. "We are done waiting," she said, her voice calm but firm. "Come with us and open the door."

Taylor braced herself for another argument, but Rafael exhaled sharply and pulled a master keycard from his pocket. Without another word, he turned and led them down the hallways toward Gia's room.

Taylor glanced at Cate, who was silent but steady, her fingers twisting the delicate silver bracelet on her wrist—an old nervous habit.

When they reached Gia's door, Rafael swiped the keycard

and gestured for them to enter, stepping back with an air of disinterest.

The room was spotless.

Too spotless.

Taylor swept her eyes over the space, her instincts kicking into overdrive. The bed was neatly made, the towels perfectly folded. The nightstand held a single empty wine glass and a half-finished bottle. No personal belongings strewn about, no sign of hurried packing.

Cate frowned, stepping toward the closet. "It looks like no one ever stayed here," she murmured.

"Housekeeping came," the manager said.

Taylor ignored the chill crawling up her spine and moved deeper into the room. Something felt off. She took in the room, processing it in her mind from a detective's frame.

And then she saw it.

The ceiling vent.

It was just slightly out of place—barely noticeable. But the way the panel was shifted just enough to leave a thin, dark gap made her stomach twist.

She pulled the chair away from the desk, centering it under the tile before she stepped up and reached, pressing her fingertips against the metal.

"There's nothing unusual there," the manager said, looking bored.

The tile shifted.

Easily.

Too easily.

A rush of cold, stale air hit her face. She glanced down at Cate. "Something's not right."

Cate moved closer, following Taylor's gaze. "What is it?"

Taylor pushed the panel all the way up, stood on her toes as high as she could and gasped. She could barely see, but above them was not a normal vent.

"It's a crawl space," she said.

A hollow silence filled the room.

Cate's face paled. "Oh my God."

"I did not have knowledge of that," Rafael said. "I'm sure it's simply to make maintenance easier."

Taylor climbed down, her heart pounding.

She turned to him. "You said the keycard logs would show if someone entered the room, right?"

"Yes," Rafael said, his voice guarded.

"But what if someone came through there?" She pointed to the ceiling. "They wouldn't trigger the electronic entry log, obviously."

Something flickered in his expression—just for a moment. A hesitation.

Cate inhaled sharply, piecing it together.

Taylor's pulse thundered. "Which means the keycard logs don't mean anything."

Brady had said the last time he saw Madison, she and Gia had been at their private pool. What if someone had been waiting? Watching?

Rafael's jaw tightened. "Señora, I assure you, this resort is safe—"

"Stop saying that!" Taylor snapped, stepping closer. "Two women are missing, and all you've done is gaslight us and act like this isn't a big deal. Look at that vent! Do you honestly expect us to believe nothing is going on?"

Rafael hesitated.

Then, to Taylor's utter disbelief, he scoffed. "Señora, perhaps they were intoxicated. It is easy to—"

"Excuse me?" Cate said, her voice dangerously calm.

Taylor felt her hands curl into fists. "You think this is their fault?"

Rafael exhaled heavily, as if they were making a problem where there wasn't one. "There are two sides to every story. Maybe your friends simply ... left."

Taylor saw red.

"Enough." She turned, pulling out her phone. "We're calling the police."

Rafael's head snapped up. "No."

Cate arched an eyebrow. "Excuse me?"

"This is not yet a police matter," Rafael said smoothly, but Taylor caught the way his jaw tightened. "And they will not come unless I give them permission."

Her breath came hot and fast. She was right to be worried about Mexico. The corrupt police department was renowned around the world. "Then start pulling security footage. Now."

He hesitated again, and that was all the confirmation Taylor needed.

He was stalling.

Before Rafael could come up with another excuse, a rapid set of footsteps echoed down the hall.

One of the bridesmaids—Ava—rushed toward them, wide-eyed and breathless. "Guys," she panted. "Last night at the reception, a bartender was hitting on Gia. Said there was a bar downtown they should check out."

Taylor's stomach dropped. "Did she go?"

Ava shook her head. "I don't know. It seemed like a casual conversation. They were laughing because he thought Gia could speak Spanish and found out she only knew a few words. He switched to English and was a nice guy. We didn't think anything of it at the time. His name tag said Daniel."

Rafael visibly tensed.

Taylor zeroed in on his reaction. "Do you know him?"

His lips pressed into a thin line. "There was no bartender named Daniel working last night."

Silence.

Cate's hand clenched at her side.

Ava's voice wavered. "But ... I saw his name tag."

Rafael slowly exhaled. "The only Daniel we have on staff works in Maintenance. And he is sixty years old."

A chill ran down Taylor's spine.

Cate whispered, "Then who was he?"

Rafael muttered something under his breath in Spanish, then turned on his heel. "I need to make a call."

Taylor grabbed his arm, forcing him to meet her gaze. "No more games. What do you know?"

For the first time, the manager looked genuinely unsettled.

"I don't know anything," he admitted. "But I have a very bad feeling."

Taylor's stomach knotted.

So did she.

And it was only getting worse.

Taylor texted Sam for an update.

His reply came quickly:

> No one has seen them. Everyone's looking now.

She texted back that she'd meet him in the lobby before turning to Cate. "Let's go."

At the lobby, Rafael spoke into his walkie-talkie, instructing security to begin a thorough search of the resort.

Ellis and Sam arrived with Brady, who looked nearly mad with fright. She couldn't imagine what he'd do when she told them about the ceiling tile.

"They weren't at the beach, and no one has seen them since last night," Sam said.

"Hey, has anyone talked to Anna?" Cate asked.

"No, and, come to think of it, I haven't seen Hazard either,"

Brady said.

One of the bridesmaids rushed into the lobby, her face flushed. "I just remembered something I need to tell you," she said breathlessly. "Last night, during the reception, one of the bartenders was flirting with Gia. He told her about some cool bar downtown they should check out later. It seemed innocent at the time, so I didn't think much of it."

"What did he look like?" Taylor asked.

"Young. Maybe mid-twenties. Mexican. Very handsome and a smooth talker."

Taylor's eyes narrowed. "Do you know his name?"

The bridesmaid paused, thinking. "His name tag said Daniel."

"That's exactly what Ava said. Daniel."

The manager, who had just returned, looked irritated. "And I'm telling you again. We don't have a bartender named Daniel," he said firmly. "The only Daniel on staff works in Maintenance, and he's at least sixty."

Chapter Six

Taylor knocked hard on Anna's door, the urgency in her movements growing stronger by the second. Cate stood beside her, arms crossed tightly, her face lined with worry.

It took a few moments before the door cracked open. Anna stood there in an oversized T-shirt, her hair messy, her eyes squinting against the hallway light. Behind her, in the dim room, Taylor spotted Hazard still sprawled across the bed, his arm flung over the side, dead to the world.

Taylor wasted no time. "Have you seen Madison or Gia?"

Anna blinked, rubbing her eyes. "What?"

"Have you seen them?" Cate pressed.

"They should be in their rooms," Anna mumbled, confused. "What's going on?"

Taylor inhaled sharply. "They're missing."

That woke her up. Anna's face paled, and she took a step back, gripping the doorframe. "What do you mean missing?"

Hazard stirred at the sound of their voices, groaning as he rolled onto his side. He squinted at them, reaching blindly for his phone on the nightstand. A moment later, he was sitting up straighter, scrolling. His expression darkened. "They never texted that they were back in their rooms."

Taylor's stomach tightened.

Anna sat down on the edge of the bed, her voice quiet, shaken. "Last night, Gia texted Hazard. She said she and Madison were going downtown, wanted to know if we wanted to join up."

Cate frowned. "Without Brady?"

Hazard sighed, running a hand through his hair. "I know it doesn't look like it for the last few days, but Brady's never been the biggest party animal. He was already passed out, and, to be honest, I figured me going with them would be enough to keep an eye on them. They said someone that Gia met was going to join up and take them to the best places. They were going whether we went or not, but I didn't want them to go alone."

Taylor crossed her arms. "And then what happened?"

Anna swallowed hard. "Hazard came to get me, and we all took an Uber to downtown Cabo. I remember seeing the bartender from the resort almost immediately. He made a beeline straight for us, all smiles, like, 'Hey! What a coincidence I found you guys!'" She let out a humorless laugh. "Yeah. Total coincidence."

"Where were you let off?" Taylor asked.

"In front of a bar called Squid Roe," he answered, rubbing his temples. "And then it all happened so fast. It was so professional. One minute we were all standing there, and—the next—they had us completely distracted."

Taylor leaned in. "Who's they?"

Hazard exhaled sharply. "A whole damn group. One guy grabbed me by the neck and shoulders, like he was just being friendly, trying to sell me drugs. Then this younger girl came up to Anna, grabbing her hand, making a fuss over her ring. She was offering to buy it."

Cate's brows furrowed. "They separated you."

Anna nodded. "Yeah. While we were busy declining them, the others must've slipped off the street with the girls. But they made it seem like we were all still together, like Madison and Gia were right behind us."

Taylor's skin prickled. "Did you see them leave?"

"No," Hazard admitted. "But, by the time we got into the bar, they were just ... gone."

Taylor clenched her jaw, forcing her mind to stay sharp. "Did they say where they were going?"

Anna nodded, her voice unsteady. "First, Gia texted that they were headed next door to Cabo Blue, but they kept moving. We were texting them while running in and out of bars looking for them, always just a step behind. Then they said the place they were in didn't have a name outside, no signs. Every time we tried to call, the connection was bad. We could barely hear them."

"What else did they say?" Taylor pressed.

Hazard sat up straighter. "They finally said they were going back to the hotel, that Gia's friend was getting them transportation."

Taylor exhaled. "And?"

Anna's hands twisted in her lap. "So we got our own cab and went straight to the resort."

"But they weren't here."

"No," Anna said, looking contrite. "Oh my God. We should've waited for them in the lobby."

Hazard looked down at his phone again, jaw tight. "Yeah, but I texted Gia to let us know when they got in their rooms. She finally texted back that they were pulling up and would see us in the morning."

Cate's fingers curled around the back of a chair. "Maybe they never actually came back."

"Damn it," Anna whispered.

The weight of it pressed against Taylor's chest. They had been in a car. Supposedly heading back. But never made it to their rooms.

Cate was right. Just because the text said they were pulling up doesn't mean they were. It could've been someone else texting from Gia's phone. Taylor's instincts were screaming at her now. Something was deeply wrong. She glanced around the room, her sharp eyes sweeping every detail. And then she saw it.

Another ceiling tile slightly off-kilter.

Her stomach dropped.

There were so many things that could happen to young women in Mexico. Kidnapping for trafficking, or for ransom. Robbery and murder. Mexico was a hot bed for criminals preying on tourists. The government tried to keep the bulk of it out of the news for fear of losing the income the foreigners brought in, but the stories were rampant throughout law enforcement.

That was why it was recommended to stay on resort grounds.

"We need to all meet up and talk about next steps," she said finally.

Her gaze lifted to the off-kilter ceiling tile again. Wide enough for someone to crawl in. She had a feeling that someone was accessing rooms through the crawl space vents, then leaving via the door, because she was willing to bet that only entry and exit through the door would trigger the electronic key card record.

Using her phone, she snapped a photo of the off kilter ceiling tile, wishing she'd also done the same in Gia's room.

Something big was happening here. Two women missing, probably in grave danger.

And it felt like they were running out of time.

Chapter Seven

Lucy had lost track of the days. Time had a way of stretching and folding in on itself when you weren't constantly on the move. For the first time in months, she wasn't watching the clock, counting hours until she had to leave, or looking over her shoulder for shadows that might not even exist.

Graham left her alone during the day. He worked—doing what, exactly, she wasn't sure. Something about remodeling houses, she thought, based on a passing comment he'd made when they'd driven past a construction site. He didn't press her to join him or explain what she did with her time, which suited her just fine. The fact that he trusted her alone in his house meant everything to her.

She spent her mornings lingering over coffee in his sunlit kitchen, flipping through the local paper or gazing out at the tidy backyard. In the afternoons, she sometimes wandered through nearby shops or sat by the canal in Bricktown, people-watching and letting her mind drift.

But the evenings were Graham's time. He'd show up just as

the sunlight began to fade, his energy still intact despite a full day's work. At first, he'd simply ask if she wanted to grab dinner, but, as the days passed, he began taking her to see the city. They'd gone to the Myriad Botanical Gardens one evening, where she'd walked through the lush greenery in silence, letting the vibrant flowers and flowing water ease some of the tension in her chest. Another evening, they'd visited the National Cowboy & Western Heritage Museum. Graham had laughed at her skeptical glances toward some of the exhibits, and she'd caught herself laughing with him—a sound she'd almost forgotten she could make.

One afternoon, Graham brought a dog home. A beagle mix with a patchy reddish coat and soulful eyes. He introduced the dog casually, explaining that he'd found it wandering near a job site and couldn't leave it behind. Lucy watched as the dog—clearly unsure of its surroundings—settled at Graham's feet like it had always belonged there.

"What's its name?" Lucy asked, crouching down to let the dog sniff her hand.

"Haven't named her yet," Graham said, scratching behind the dog's ears. "Figured she'd let me know when I got it right."

Lucy's throat tightened as she thought of Ginger, her own dog she'd left behind in Georgia. The dog reminded her so much of Ginger—the same quiet resilience, the same way she leaned into a gentle touch. Lucy wondered, not for the first time, if Ginger was okay. If she missed her as much as Lucy missed her.

"What about Ginger?"

He lit up. "I like that. Ginger, it is."

She hid her delight. Having another Ginger around would help ease the loneliness for the dog she'd left behind.

Tonight, Graham had taken her to a cozy, unassuming

barbecue joint he claimed was the best in town. It was a dog-friendly place tucked away in a quiet neighborhood, the kind of diner that locals guarded jealously from tourists. They sat at a wooden table outside, the scent of smoked meat and tangy sauce filling the air.

Lucy poked at her pulled pork sandwich, watching as Graham would expertly dismantle a plate of ribs, take a bite himself then pass a bit down to Ginger.

"You've got sauce on your face," she said, smirking.

Graham grinned and wiped at his cheek with a napkin. "Occupational hazard," he said. "You can't eat barbecue without getting a little messy."

Lucy shook her head but couldn't suppress her smile. There was something disarming about him, a warmth she wasn't used to. It didn't hurt that he never pushed her to share anything about herself. He seemed perfectly content to exist in the moment, letting their conversations drift from light banter to idle observations about the places they visited.

"You don't talk much about yourself," Lucy said, surprising even herself with the statement. She hadn't meant to pry, but something about the easy rhythm of their evenings made her curious.

Graham set down his rib, wiping his hands on a napkin before leaning back in his chair. "Not much to tell," he said lightly. But there was a shadow in his eyes that said otherwise.

"I doubt that," she said. "Nobody gets to your age without a few stories."

He held his heart dramatically. "My age? Ouch. I'm sure I'm not that much older than you."

"I'm thirty-four."

He chuckled. "Fair enough. On that note, let me skip the age thing. You want the abridged version of my shit story—um ... I mean, my history?"

She nodded, leaning forward slightly. She was surprisingly curious.

He took a sip of his sweet tea before speaking. "I was born just over the state line in a tiny Kansas town, but I always preferred Oklahoma City. Middle class, nothing fancy, but I wasn't always as settled as I seem now. Left home when I was seventeen. My dad and I ... didn't see eye to eye. Figured I'd make my own way."

"Where'd you go?" she asked, genuinely intrigued.

"Everywhere," he said with a faint smile. "Started out in Colorado. Snowboarding, working odd jobs at ski resorts. When the snow melted, I'd head west. Spent a couple of years surfing in California, waiting tables to pay the bills. Did a stint in Montana working on a dude ranch. Spent some time in Florida, fishing and fixing boats. You name it, I probably tried it."

Lucy raised an eyebrow. "And now you remodel houses? That's quite a leap."

"Yeah, well, life has a way of throwing you curveballs," he said, his tone shifting. He stared at his glass for a moment before continuing. "Met a woman in California. Her name was Sara. She was ... she was something else. Smart, funny, beautiful. We got married, had a daughter who was the spitting image of Sara. Named her Anna, and she was the most amazing thing that had ever happened to either of us. Anna changed everything. She was the sun that we orbited around."

Lucy's breath caught. She almost remarked that Anna was her sister's name but stopped herself just in time. Something about the way his voice softened around the name made her instinctively hold back. What he was telling wasn't easy for him.

"When Anna was six, she got sick. First a simple cold. Then it turned into pneumonia." He paused, his jaw tightening. "It hit her hard and, before we could think straight, she was on a ventilator. We still thought she'd pull through, but ... she didn't."

Lucy's chest ached at the raw pain in his voice. She didn't know what to say, so she said nothing.

"Sara and I tried to hold it together, but we couldn't," he continued. "We were both so lost in our own grief, there was no room for each other. So, I came back here. Figured I'd start over, build something solid for once in my life."

"I'm sorry," Lucy said softly. "About Anna. And Sara."

He nodded, his gaze distant. "Thanks. It's been a few years. Doesn't hurt any less, but you learn to carry it."

Lucy studied him, wondering how someone could endure that kind of loss and still have room to care for a stranger like her.

"What about you?" he asked, his eyes meeting hers. "You've got that same look I used to have. Like you're running from something."

She forced a smile. "Like you said, not much to tell."

He didn't push, just nodded and picked up another rib. But Lucy could feel his words lingering, their weight pressing against the carefully constructed walls she'd built around herself. For a moment, as she watched him share his meal with the rescue dog at his feet, she wondered what it would be like to be married to a man like Graham. A nice guy. Someone who led such a simple, relaxed life.

The thought made her chest tighten, and she looked away, focusing on her plate. She couldn't afford to think like that. Not now. Not ever.

He wiped his mouth and set his napkin down.

"I just need you to answer one question, Lily," he said solemnly. "I've been doing a lot of thinking, and I have to know."

She felt panic rise in her throat. What did he want to know? Was this where they would have to part?

"Okay," she said tentatively.

"Red is obviously not your color so just what the hell color hair do you really have?"

They laughed, and her body relaxed with relief.

Chapter Eight

When the room spins, someone has to step up to steady it. Taylor didn't necessarily want the weight, but she knew how to carry it. The air in the hotel's conference room was thick with tension and the smell of stale coffee. They were well into the afternoon now and no progress made. Taylor sat at the head of the table, her back straight, hands clasped together. As much as she hated to be in this position, she knew she was the best equipped to handle this. Her training, her experience—they'd all naturally put her in charge.

It was a glass half full sort of experience. Yes, she'd wanted to go back to work, but not like this. Not with her own family and in a country where crime and corruption were sure to impede any sort of real investigation.

Right now, she felt at a loss.

Brady sat between his two brothers, his knee bouncing under the table. He looked hollowed out, like every ounce of energy had been drained from his body and been replaced with nothing but pure, exhausting fear. His brothers and Hazard had gone back downtown, looking everywhere that was open, asking questions, and going down every back alley they could find.

They'd turned up nothing.

Some of the bridal party members were still there.

Anna and Hazard sat opposite Cate and Ellis, looking just as weary. And then there was Aunt Heidi—arms crossed, glaring daggers at Hazard every time she looked his way. She'd been the last one informed about the girls being gone, and she wasn't taking that lightly either.

At the front of the room, the official from the Mexican police department, a broad-shouldered man with graying temples named Inspector Alvarez, adjusted the sleeves of his uniform. His expression was unreadable, but Taylor had already caught the dismissiveness in his tone earlier. Upon first laying eyes on them, he carried an aura of distaste for Americans.

And then there was the resort manager, Rafael, standing near the wall like he wanted to be anywhere but there. His arms were crossed tightly over his chest, his mouth set in a defensive line. He'd nearly had to be strong-armed into bringing the police in.

Inspector Alvarez cleared his throat. "We have spoken to security staff, reviewed keycard logs, and conducted an initial search. As of now, there is no evidence that anything happened on the grounds of the hotel." His gaze flicked briefly to Rafael, as if reassuring him.

Rafael exhaled through his nose. "Exactly. There is nothing to suggest this resort is involved."

Taylor clenched her jaw. "That's because they weren't taken from the hotel. They were taken after being lured downtown from someone who claims to work here."

The mysterious Daniel, who Rafael declared didn't exist.

Alvarez raised a hand as if to settle the conversation before it escalated. "Señora, let us be clear—this was a risk they took.

They chose to go downtown; they chose to drink. These cases are unfortunate, but they are not uncommon. We never encourage visitors to galivant around town after dark, but yet, they do. Let me ask you, was either woman wearing expensive jewelry?"

Brady slammed his hands on the table. They'd already discussed earlier that Madison's huge new wedding ring was gone, and they assumed it was on her hand. He looked livid. "Are you seriously blaming them?"

Heidi scoffed, shaking her head. "Typical that you would let her do something dangerous like this, Brady. You shouldn't have gone to sleep before Madison came in." She turned her glare back to Hazard. "And you went along with it! What were you thinking?"

Hazard exhaled sharply. "I thought I was keeping an eye on them."

"Well, you failed!"

"Enough." Taylor's voice cut through the room like a blade. She turned back to Alvarez. "Blaming them isn't getting us anywhere. We need to know what's being done."

Alvarez straightened. "The reality is, we have limited resources. Our department handles hundreds of missing persons reports, and unless there is evidence of a crime—"

"Evidence?" Cate's voice was sharp with disbelief. "They were taken. They never returned to the resort! That's the evidence!"

Alvarez exhaled as if this was exhausting for him. "I fully believe they'll show up soon but, in the meantime, we are monitoring leads. We will continue to investigate, but there is no reason to assume—"

A sharp knock at the door cut him off.

Everyone froze.

Then Sam stood, moving to open it.

A tall, serious-looking man stepped inside, a lanyard with a government badge around his neck. His navy-blue suit was crisp, and he carried an air of quiet authority.

"I'm Ryan Davis, from the U.S. Consulate," he introduced himself, nodding politely. "I understand you have two American citizens missing?"

Alvarez immediately tensed. "This is a local matter. How did you—"

"I called him," Sam said, his voice steely.

Taylor felt a rush of pride.

Ryan didn't even blink. He pulled out a folder and flipped it open. "By some reports, there are more than 100,000 missing persons in Mexico," he said, his voice even. "Currently, around five hundred and fifty of those are Americans. Unfortunately, every missing person's case is considered part of ongoing investigations, which means you won't be able to access any information from government sites."

Brady inhaled sharply. Cate's hands curled into fists.

Ryan continued, "You aren't missing much. There's no centralized system like NAMUS or The Charley Project. The closest thing we have for Mexico is grassroots efforts—families who keep lists of missing loved ones and personally go searching for them. Some even unearth mass graves." His voice darkened. "It's a hard job. Especially with crime gangs rampant and the government largely ... uninterested."

Alvarez's face reddened. "That is not true. We take missing persons seriously."

Ryan looked at him, unimpressed. "Do you?"

"I obtained the copies of their passports from Mr. Rafael here, didn't I? I currently have someone in town making flyers from the photos," he replied.

"What else? Have you turned over every room, bed, and corner of the grounds of this property? Have you lent every possible officer to the search? Have you met with every member of your staff, and did you call us as soon as you knew you had a missing Americans case on your hands? Oh wait—you never called at all, did you? I'm only here now because of Samuel Stone." He gestured at Sam.

Alvarez let out a sharp breath and pushed his chair back. "I will not sit here and be insulted." Without another word, he turned on his heel and stormed out.

Silence filled the room.

Ryan shrugged. "Not a big loss. The local police will do everything they can to be an obstacle in an investigation like this."

"Why?" Ellis asked.

Taylor leaned back, rubbing her temples. "This is insane. How is this even happening at a five-star resort, and why are the local police so hard to work with?"

Ryan closed his folder. "Because it would look bad for the resort. Hurt them in the wallet, so they work out deals with police to keep investigations minimized. Legal answer, it's the system. If things were going to change, they'd have to change the constitution."

Cate shook her head. "That's impossible."

Ryan's gaze was grim. "And, honestly, some cases are so deeply entangled with cartels that people would rather do nothing than risk their lives."

The room was heavy with quiet understanding.

Sam, who had been typing furiously on his laptop, suddenly looked up. "To update you all on my search, I still haven't found much ... but I was able to access Interpol's national police website. When the site actually works," he muttered, "you can look at yellow notices—missing persons alerts. You can even filter by country. I put in Mexico and cross-referenced with the

U.S. as a likely country of visitation, and a ton of cases popped up."

Taylor sat up straighter. "That's something."

Sam shrugged. "It's not user-friendly though. And it seems like it's meant for much later in cases, not in the first few days."

Taylor nodded. "Still, Sam, good job. It's better than nothing."

Ryan set his hands on the table. "Okay. We need to establish next steps. The police aren't going to do much, so it's up to you to push for action."

Taylor exhaled. "Alright. Here's what I think we should do next."

Chapter Nine

Lucy woke with a start, her heart pounding and her pulse racing as if she'd been running in her sleep. The faint, scuttling sound she'd heard in the night still lingered in her mind. Mice, maybe. Or something else. She shivered and made a mental note to ask Graham about it later, though the thought of bringing it up—even casually—made her feel oddly self-conscious. Everything about him screamed competence and control. She didn't want to seem like she couldn't handle a mouse.

She rubbed her hands over her arms, trying to shake off the jittery energy that had been following her since she opened her eyes. Her gaze swept the room: tidy, understated, warm in its simplicity. Just like him. Graham was gone—off to work, she assumed—and the quiet of the house pressed against her chest.

"He's a nice guy," she murmured to herself, the words barely audible in the stillness. It wasn't an argument or a realization. It was just a fact. The kind of man you don't meet often, who offers kindness without strings. And yet, she'd been here long enough to know that "nice" didn't mean safe. Nice didn't mean she shouldn't keep her guard up.

Unable to sit still, Lucy threw on her sweatshirt and pants, then wandered out of the guest room and into the hall. The house was quiet except for the faint hum of the refrigerator. Ginger trailed behind her, her nails clicking softly on the hardwood floor.

Lucy paused at the kitchen counter, her fingers brushing over a small stack of mail. She glanced at the envelopes, her breath catching when she saw his name. She knew she shouldn't—she knew it—but her hands moved on their own, flipping through the pile. Bills, a postcard from someone named "Jim," in Montana, a flyer for a local hardware store. Nothing out of the ordinary. Beneath the stack, however, was a roll of cash. Her pulse quickened as she picked it up, her fingers brushing over the crisp bills. She couldn't help but wonder why he'd leave something like this out in the open.

She held it for a second, then set it back and arranged the mail the way she'd found it. Her nerves buzzed as she moved through the house. The living room was cozy, the shelves lined with books and small trinkets. She stopped in front of a framed photo on the mantel: Graham with his arm around a woman.

His ex-wife, she assumed.

She was pretty in an understated way, her smile warm and open. Lucy's chest tightened, a mix of jealousy and something darker—a nagging feeling that this woman had known a side of Graham that Lucy never would.

She moved on, her steps light as if she didn't want the house to hear her. When she reached his bedroom, she hesitated. The door was ajar, an invitation she wasn't sure she should accept. But the tension in her chest pushed her forward. She stepped inside, her eyes immediately drawn to the neatly made bed and the stack of photo albums on the dresser.

Lucy picked up the top album, her fingers trembling slightly as she opened it. She took it to the bed and sat cross-legged with

Ginger curling up beside her. She could smell the light scent of Graham's woodsy cologne as she flipped through the pages.

The first few photos were of him and his ex-wife on their wedding day. It was a church wedding, and they looked happy, glowing with the kind of love Lucy had only seen in movies. She reminded Lucy of a young Barbara Streisand. Untamed curly hair and a nose that was just different enough to give her an understated and unusual beauty. Lucy turned the page, and the photos shifted to their travels: the two of them in hiking gear, standing in front of waterfalls and mountains. Then one picture stopped her cold. They were standing in front of a massive building with a gleaming gold dome. The caption read: "State Museum St. Isaac's Cathedral."

Lucy frowned. It looked very different than any kind of building she'd ever seen. She flipped the page, her unease growing. There was a photo of Graham with his hand on his wife's swollen belly, both laughing. Then came the pictures of their daughter, Anna. As a baby, then a toddler, her big, bright eyes staring straight at the camera. More photos of Graham holding her on his chest, sleeping contentedly. One shot caught him smiling up at the camera, a peaceful and joyful grin as he held his child.

A child that would soon be ripped away from him by a crazy new virus that no one saw coming. Lucy's throat tightened, and her fingers trembled as she turned another page. But there was nothing. Just blank spaces where photos should have been.

Her mind raced as she flipped back to the photo of the cathedral. She stared at it, the gold dome burning into her thoughts. Ginger whined again, and Lucy absently scratched behind her ears.

She set the album aside and crossed to Graham's desk. His laptop sat closed, and she hesitated only for a moment before flipping it open. She typed "State Museum St. Isaac's Cathedral" into the search bar and hit enter.

Her heart dropped when the results loaded. Russia. The cathedral was in St. Petersburg. Her hands began to shake as her mind spiraled. Russia. Ukraine. Could Graham have connections there? What if it wasn't a coincidence she'd ended up in his house? What if he'd been sent by Ian's Ukrainian family to find her and take Johnny?

She slammed the laptop shut and glanced out the window, her breath quick and shallow. A man on a bike pedaled leisurely down the street, his face hidden by the brim of his cap. Lucy froze, her paranoia kicking into overdrive. Was he watching the house? Was he waiting for her to make a move? What if he came back?

She yanked the curtains closed and backed away, her pulse roaring in her ears. Ginger followed her, whining insistently, but Lucy barely noticed. After she pulled her sneakers on, she grabbed her duffel bag from the guest room and started throwing her clothes into it. Her movements were frantic, driven by the need to go.

As she zipped up the bag, her mind flashed back to the roll of cash on the kitchen counter. It would be so easy to take it. Graham would never know it was her. But then she thought about the way he'd been so good to her—offering her a place to stay, asking for nothing in return. The guilt twisted in her stomach, and she shook her head. She couldn't do that to him, not after everything.

Still, the realization hit her hard: she'd have to make her cash stretch. She still couldn't risk going into a bank or leaving any kind of electronic trail with her credit cards.

At the last minute, she crouched down and hugged Ginger, her breath hitching. "You're coming with me," she whispered, her voice trembling. She grabbed the dog's food bowls and leash, stuffing them into the duffel.

Ginger wagged her tail, oblivious to the chaos unfolding around her.

Lucy carried her bag and led Ginger out to the Jeep, throwing everything into the back seat before she helped the dog in. When she climbed into the driver's seat, her hands gripped the wheel so tightly her knuckles turned white.

With a deep breath, she started the engine and peeled out of the driveway, the tires squealing as she sped down the street.

Her heart pounded as she drove, the fear chasing her like a shadow. She didn't know where she was going, but she knew one thing for certain: she had to keep moving. If they were following her, they couldn't find out she didn't have Johnny. And she couldn't afford to trust anyone. Not even Graham.

Chapter Ten

Taylor lay on the bed fully clothed, her limbs heavy with exhaustion, yet her mind spun in relentless circles. Sam was beside her, one arm draped over his forehead, his breathing slow but not deep enough to be asleep. Neither of them had the luxury of rest—not when two people they cared about had vanished into the darkness, swallowed up by something too sinister to name yet.

They had agreed to get a few hours of sleep before meeting back in the war room, but it was a joke. Sleep was impossible. Every time she closed her eyes, the last images of Madison and Gia—laughing, carefree, alive—flashed behind her eyelids.

The look of foreboding and fear etched on Ellis' face.

Her phone rested on her stomach, screen dark but ready. They all had their phones within reach, waiting. What if there was a ransom call?

She exhaled sharply, pressing the heels of her hands into her eyes.

Think, Taylor.

Her notepad lay open on the nightstand, scribbled with

notes. She grabbed the pen, flipping back through her hastily-written bullet points.

- **Rafael had reviewed the security footage but hasn't let them see it. Footage shows: Girls leaving Madison's room → Going to Gia's room → Walking to lobby → Walking out resort gate → Waiting area for Ubers → Off-camera.**
- **Why hasn't he let us see it ourselves?**
- **Could he be hiding something?**
- **Anna had called every urgent care and hospital in the area. Nothing.**

She tapped the pen against the paper, her knee bouncing.

Sam sighed beside her, adjusting his pillow. "You need to shut your brain off for a little while."

Taylor snorted. "Not happening."

He rolled onto his side, propping himself on his elbow. "I found something earlier."

Her stomach twisted at his tone. "Do I want to know?"

He hesitated. "Probably not."

Taylor sat up, swinging her legs over the side of the bed. "Tell me."

Sam sighed, grabbing his laptop from the nightstand and flipping it open. The screen glowed eerily in the dim room. "There was a case recently ... Nine students. Found on the side of a local highway. A bag of dismembered hands nearby."

Taylor's stomach turned. "I heard about that. But ... not Americans, right?"

"No," he admitted. "But there was another case recently—two Australians and one American. The bodies were recovered from a remote well—about fifty feet deep. They think that the thieves who killed them wanted their truck. The bodies were dumped near the coast." He glanced up at her, voice quieter.

She inhaled sharply, pressing her fingers to her temples.

Sam hesitated. "In 2021, there were 300 to 400 kidnappings of American citizens in Mexico. In 2023, it was 463. Seems to be a recurring security issue."

Taylor dropped her head into her hands.

"God, I hope Ellis isn't seeing these internet stories."

Sam nodded grimly. "I doubt he's looking. Aunt Heidi is, no doubt. She's called everyone back home too. No one's heard from the girls."

Taylor let out a slow breath, rolling her shoulders back. Keep moving. Focus. "What about the visibility efforts?"

He'd taken that much off her plate, and she felt thankful for his help.

"I've compiled everything. Pictures, details, times. I already reached out to local journalists and posted across social media. And I emailed CNN and Fox, hoping to get international coverage."

She looked up, a flicker of gratitude in her exhausted gaze. "Good. That's all good." She jotted it down in her bullet points. Her fingers tightened around the pen. "So, we know now that Gia's passport wasn't in her safe, but Madison's was still in her room." She frowned, processing it. "I thought everyone would put theirs in the safe. So why would Gia take her passport with her, knowing they were just going to drink?"

Sam sat up, mirroring her concern. "Hard to understand. Unless *she* didn't take it. Maybe someone else took it. Someone may have gotten into her room and knew how to open the safe."

Taylor swallowed hard.

Cate and Ellis had questioned staff about Daniel, the so-called bartender. Nothing. Either no one spoke enough English, or they were lying.

Taylor rubbed her temples. "I don't buy it. Someone must have seen him. He was standing there at the reception, acting like staff, and no one noticed he wasn't real?"

Sam leaned forward, his elbows resting on his knees. "What if the staff wasn't lying?"

Taylor blinked.

He looked at her, serious. "What if they did see him ... and they're covering for him?"

Her stomach tightened. "You think the whole resort is involved?"

He shrugged. "Maybe not all of them. But someone is. The vent access in the rooms. The faked staff member. The security footage we haven't seen ourselves? That's a lot of coincidences."

Taylor's pulse thudded against her ribs.

A low buzzing filled the air.

Sam's phone.

He checked it. "Gia's parents just landed. They're heading here now."

Taylor stood abruptly, rolling her shoulders back. "I can't sit here. I must do something. And they're going to want to talk to someone about what we've done so far. I'll wait in the lobby."

Sam exhaled. "Taylor, you're running on fumes."

"I don't care." She turned to him, determination flashing in her eyes. "You know what? Why don't you wait in the lobby? I'm going down to the police station. Right now."

Sam rubbed his face. "Taylor—"

"No." She cut him off. "They aren't moving fast enough. I need to push them."

Brady's words from earlier echoed in her mind.

"And if the police won't help?"

Taylor clenched her jaw, gripping the doorknob.

"Then we find them ourselves."

Chapter Eleven

Taylor pressed send on her phone, messaging Ellis to meet Gia's parents in the lobby when they arrived. The moment the text showed delivered, she slid her phone into her bag and took a deep breath.

"You ready?" Sam asked quietly. He'd told her he wasn't about to lose her, too, and she wasn't going alone anywhere in Mexico.

He'd obviously forgotten that she could take care of herself. But now wasn't the time to assert her independence. She was glad he was going. Turns out that Sam has a natural ability for investigation, thinking of things to do that most non-LEOs—law enforcement officers—didn't.

They made a good team.

When they walked through the sprawling resort, the air already thick with humidity despite the early morning hour, the lavish grounds felt like an entirely different world compared to the reality they were heading toward. Guests in crisp linen outfits sipped coffee under the palapas, completely unaware of the nightmare unfolding beneath the surface of this picturesque paradise.

Once again, she couldn't wait to get her feet back onto the red Georgia clay, within the gates of the farm. She'd tried to push thoughts of Lennon out of her mind multiple times already that day. Right now, she needed to focus on finding Madison and Gia.

Outside the gated entrance, a white van sat idling, its paint job so pristine it practically sparkled under the sun. If it wasn't so perfectly clean, Taylor might have found it suspicious.

Sam must have been thinking the same thing because he muttered, "If this thing was the least bit dingy, I'd swear it was a setup."

Taylor shot him a dry look before stepping toward the vehicle. The driver, a broad-shouldered man with salt-and-pepper hair and a kind smile, rolled down the window. "Taylor?"

"That's me," she confirmed.

He nodded. "I'm Manuel. Welcome to Cabo."

Taylor and Sam climbed into the van, the doors clicking shut behind them as Manuel pulled onto the main road, leaving the resort behind. As they drove, the scenery changed drastically. The pristine beaches and five-star hotels gave way to stretches of dry, rocky land. Cabo wasn't the lush, tropical paradise most tourists imagined—it was a desert, at least until you reached the city or the beaches.

They passed jagged mountains, their slopes dotted with makeshift homes, some barely standing, hidden high up within the ridges. Further down, bridges loomed overhead, with tattered tents lined beneath them—clusters of the unseen, the forgotten.

Taylor watched the landscape in silence, her stomach twisting.

"So," Manuel said after a few moments, looking at them in the mirror. "Where are you from?"

"Georgia," Taylor answered, and Sam nodded beside her.

Manuel's face lit up. "I used to live in Georgia. A long time ago."

"Really?" she asked, surprised.

He nodded. "Sure did. Worked for a landscaping company. I stayed there for five years. Hard work, but I made good money." A hint of pride entered his voice. "I have two sons in the U.S. now—both in college."

"That's great," Sam said genuinely.

"And one small daughter here," Manuel added, a softer smile touching his lips. "She's the one who really keeps me busy."

Taylor liked him. He felt ... safe. Or, at least, safer than anyone else they'd spoken to in the last twenty-four hours.

She hesitated, then asked, "Manuel, has Cabo ever had trouble with the cartel?"

The question shifted the air in the van.

Manuel fell silent, gripping the steering wheel a little tighter. Then, without looking at her, he lifted a hand and gestured toward the mountains. "The cartel are always around," he said evenly. "But they usually leave the tourists alone."

Usually.

The word sank into Taylor's gut like a lead weight. She turned slightly, locking eyes with Sam. His face mirrored her worry.

She forced herself to keep her voice light. "I read that the cartel in this part of Mexico is involved in trafficking deadly drugs," she said, hoping to keep him talking.

Manuel met her eyes through the rearview mirror, and this time there was a warning in them. "Asking about the cartel can get you into some trouble, ma'am." His voice was gentle, but firm. "I'd hate to see you get hurt."

Sam shifted beside her, nudging her knee. A silent message —drop it.

Taylor cleared her throat. "I'm sorry. I didn't mean anything by it."

Manuel said nothing for a few more miles. The road stretched before them, leading deeper into the city, where buildings clustered together in a chaotic blend of color and age.

Finally, he sighed, glancing at them again. "Do you have trouble?"

Taylor hesitated.

"Why are you going to the police station?" he added.

She exhaled. No more dancing around it. "Yes, we have big trouble. Two of our friends are missing. Two young women. Last seen downtown and never made it back to the resort."

Manuel's hands tightened on the wheel. "The bars downtown are not good for women to go alone." He shook his head. "But it's usually just a shakedown."

Sam frowned. "What do you mean?"

Manuel glanced at them again, his expression grave. "Most common thing I hear? Servers will take money for each round of drinks, but, when the guests try to leave, they get a second bill. The first payments? Pocketed. And since tourists don't ask for receipts, they must pay again."

Taylor considered it. "It's a scam, then."

"Yes. But ..." He sighed. "If your friends are missing, it's probably not that simple."

"They're saying the girls weren't even there," Sam added, his jaw tight. "Like they never existed."

Manuel's expression darkened.

"The police won't do anything," Taylor continued.

Manuel was quiet for a moment. Then, finally, he asked, "Would you like my help?"

Taylor froze.

Sam turned to her, brows raised in question.

Taylor's first instinct was to wonder if this was a shakedown.

Every Little Thing

He could take them all over the city, driving in circles, pretending to help while wasting time. But then again ... Alvarez wasn't helping. Rafael wasn't helping.

And if Manuel was telling the truth—if he'd lived in Cabo for years, had roots here—maybe he actually could help them navigate a system stacked against them.

Sam gave her a questioning look. He wanted her to decide.

"Yes," she said firmly. "Actually, we'd love that, Manuel."

Chapter Twelve

Cabo San Lucas during the day was nothing like the glossy brochures or Instagram reels that sold the fantasy to foreigners, far and wide. Sure, there was still sunlight glinting off parked mopeds, vibrant murals splashed across cracked stucco walls, and palm trees waving lazily in the breeze—but down here, in the tangle of downtown streets, it all felt edgier. Grittier.

More real.

Manuel pulled the van up to the curb in front of a narrow building wedged between a closed pharmacy and a souvenir shop stacked with straw hats and beaded jewelry.

"Slim's Elbow Room," he said, nodding toward the door. "Start here."

Taylor and Sam stepped out, greeted by the sudden blast of heat. The sidewalk was narrow and uneven. They exchanged a look, then pushed open the faded wooden door beneath the rusty sign.

Inside was dim, cool, and tiny. The bar barely had enough space for six people shoulder to shoulder. The air smelled like decades of spilled tequila and cigarette smoke that lingered in the wood like secrets.

A "CASH ONLY" sign hung crookedly above the counter. Behind the bar, a wall of liquor bottles gleamed under a string of mismatched holiday lights. A short, smiling man with a thick accent greeted them warmly. "Want something strong or something dangerous?"

Taylor smiled faintly but kept it professional. "We're looking for two girls. Tourists. They may have been in here last night. Do you remember them?"

She showed him pictures of Madison and Gia on her phone.

He squinted, then shrugged. "I don't think so. But everyone looks the same after two margaritas." He laughed at his own joke, then got distracted by a regular flagging him down for another round.

They didn't linger.

Back in the van, Manuel was already in motion again.

Their next stop was Happy Ending Cantina, a larger place that straddled the line between beachy dive and spring break cliché.

Taylor stared at the neon pink lettering above the bar and muttered to Sam, "This sounds more like a massage parlor in Vegas than a cantina."

He chuckled under his breath. "If they start handing out robes, I'm leaving."

Inside, music thumped from overhead speakers while a scattering of tourists nursed beers and tried to look like they belonged. Manuel spoke quietly with a waitress in the corner while Taylor scanned the room. No sign of the girls. Just more strangers, more dead ends.

The third stop—El Squid Roe—was sensory overload. Part nightclub, part dance hall, part neon-lit funhouse. The moment they stepped through the door, Taylor's eyes were pulled toward a loud commotion near the back.

A group of four Americans—early twenties, she guessed—were red-faced and yelling at a manager who stood his ground with crossed arms.

"We already paid for those!" one of the women shouted, waving a crumpled stack of pesos in her hand.

"You pay when you leave," the manager insisted.

"That was three rounds ago!" her friend snapped.

Taylor remembered Manuel's words from earlier. Double billing. No receipts. No proof.

Corruption wrapped in alcohol haze.

She nudged Sam. "This is exactly what he warned us about."

He nodded grimly. "Our daughters are never coming to Mexico for spring break."

"Not even over my dead body," Taylor agreed, wondering how they could keep Alice and Lennon safe forever.

They left without asking questions—the scene was already spiraling into another language, with threats of calling police and tourists pulling out translation apps.

On their way back to the van, they were swarmed by a group of children no older than eight or nine, holding woven bracelets and paper flowers, shouting "Mira! Mira!" and tugging gently at their sleeves.

Taylor knelt instinctively, brushing one child's cheek with her hand. Dirt smudged her forehead, and her sandals were held together by ratty string.

"They shouldn't be out here alone," she murmured to Sam.

"I don't think they have another option," he replied softly. "They call them chicklettes. The ring leaders—their coyotes—send them out to beg. They don't keep a penny for themselves."

She shook her head.

Next, they stopped briefly outside Bikini Bar, but Manuel advised them to wait in the van. "Let me try it without you."

Taylor sweated inside the van, the air now stifling despite the open windows. Her phone buzzed repeatedly—texts from Cate, Ellis, Aunt Heidi, even Ryan checking in. Still no word on Madison or Gia.

Ellis had contacted a reporter in Georgia, and she'd promised to do a pitch to her boss, and hopefully would run a segment on their evening news. If they were lucky, Atlanta might pick it up.

Finally, as the sun began to dip lower in the sky, casting a golden glow over the stucco walls and dusty streets, Manuel turned off the main road and onto a narrow, uneven lane.

"Where are we going?" Taylor asked, her heart rate kicking up.

"There's one more place," he said.

The van rolled to a stop in front of a dilapidated building at the end of a secluded alley. The windows were barred. A rickety wooden staircase led to a door with peeling green paint and no sign.

"I need to go in alone here too," Manuel said. He scowled. "Don't unlock the doors for anyone. And ... I need some money."

Taylor and Sam exchanged a look.

She didn't answer immediately. She studied Manuel's eyes —clear, steady. His voice hadn't changed, not even once today, but something felt different. Yet, to be honest, Alvarez had given them nothing. If this was a scam, it was a much smarter one than any she'd seen so far.

She reached into her bag, pulled out a few folded bills, and handed them over.

He looked at the bills and shook his head. "Not enough."

Sam handed over a twenty. "Don't make us regret this," he said.

Manuel nodded once, then stepped out of the van and jogged up the creaking staircase. He knocked once, paused, then knocked twice more before the door cracked open and he slipped inside.

Taylor stared at the building, every muscle in her body tense. It infuriated her that they had to stoop to bribery, simply because the local police force didn't want to put in any effort.

Minutes passed. Ten. Then fifteen.

"What if he doesn't come back?" Sam asked.

She didn't answer.

Chapter Thirteen

Taylor stared into the darkness beyond the windshield, her thoughts scattering in a hundred directions. This sure wasn't turning out to be the vacation that everyone told her she'd needed.

A last reprieve of recovery before going back to her job. Long days lounging on the beach, listening to the waves.

She nearly laughed. It couldn't be any further from that fantasy. Not only that, but it was making her remember the things about her job that she disliked, like the occasional crooked cop that crossed her path. There were a lot of good guys in law enforcement, but there was always going to be a bad apple in the bunch.

In Mexico, it felt like the whole bushel was rotten.

"Are you okay?" Sam asked, taking her hand in his and squeezing. "I think you're pushing yourself too hard. I don't want you to relapse."

"I'm fine." She was exhausted—mentally, emotionally, physically—but there was no room for rest. Not yet. Not until Madison and Gia were found. Not until they were safe.

The van sat parked behind a closed hardware shop, its corrugated metal door rattling occasionally in the wind. The distant hum of traffic, the flicker of a single light on the side of the building, and the faint sound of a dog barking in the distance were the only signs of life.

Sam sat beside her in the passenger seat, scrolling silently through his phone, his brow furrowed in concentration.

Manuel had disappeared twenty minutes ago, walking up a rickety stairway and through an unmarked door. Every minute that passed stretched longer than the last.

Taylor leaned her head back against the seat, trying to breathe through the anxiety clawing at her chest.

She turned slightly to look at Sam. "Do you think Lennon's okay?"

He blinked, startled by the sudden change in topic, then softened. "Yeah. Of course. She's with Jo, remember? She's probably asleep in that little sleep sack you insist on her using even though it's at least 80 degrees in Georgia."

Taylor smiled weakly. "She always kicks her way out of it by midnight."

He chuckled. "I bet she's doing that thing where she lifts one chubby leg up and slams it down like a baby wrestler."

Taylor laughed, the sound catching in her throat. "I miss her. And Alice."

"I know," Sam said. He reached over and laced his fingers through hers. "Me too. And Johnny, of course."

Taylor stared down at their hands. "If something ever happened to me ..."

"Don't," Sam said gently but firmly. "Don't go there."

"But look at what we're doing, Sam. We're sitting in a dark alley in a city we don't know, chasing after leads from someone we barely know, hoping to rescue two women who were taken by criminals who might have ties to something much bigger. It's —insane."

"It is," he admitted. "But the alternative is to do nothing. You know we can't do that either. For Ellis' sake if nothing else."

She pressed her free hand to her chest, grounding herself in the rhythm of her breath. "It's so damn scary. I just keep thinking, what if this was Lennon someday? Traveling with friends, trusting the wrong person, and disappearing?"

Sam's jaw tightened. "Then I pray to God someone like you is out there, doing whatever it takes to bring her home."

She had another worry pulsing through her. One she hadn't said out loud yet. But then he seemed to read her mind, like he always did.

"Switching subjects," Sam said, "but have you heard from Lucy?"

She turned to him, brows lifting. "No. And I've been trying not to think about it with everything else going on, but—" she hesitated, voice lowering, "—my gut's saying it's more than her usual running away from her problems, that something's not right with her. And when that happens ..."

He looked at her, his face darkening. "You're rarely wrong."

Taylor exhaled slowly. "What if, like Madison and Gia, she got tangled up with the wrong people? What if she's in trouble too?"

"We'll find her when we get back," Sam said quietly, though his tone lacked the usual certainty. "Help her get into treatment again. We'll insist harder this time that she stay with it."

"Sounds easier than it will be. We both know that convincing someone with a mental illness that they are mentally ill is near to impossible. I just hope she doesn't keep unravelling until it's too late to get her back."

The silence that followed was thick with unspoken fears.

The only positive thing was that at least Lucy wasn't in Mexico where a person could disappear without a trace and authorities didn't care.

Then, finally—footsteps.

Manuel reappeared, emerging from the shadows like a ghost. As he approached the van, she saw it on his face before he said a word. Something had changed.

He opened the driver's side door and slid inside, glancing at both before speaking. The engine rumbled to life, humming low and steady. It felt like a heartbeat.

"My contact," Manuel began, "used to be with the federales. Now he keeps an ear to the street. He says there's been talk—two foreign girls taken last night. Not a cartel job. Not human trafficking. A local crew. Criminals who know how to work the tourists."

Taylor nodded slowly, her pulse starting to thrum louder.

"They get them drunk, charm them—sending in someone like your 'Daniel.' Put them in a car, take them out somewhere remote, scare them, demand money. Then they bring them back before morning. Quick cash. No paperwork. No missing person reports."

Taylor's voice was razor sharp. "But that didn't happen this time. They didn't bring them back."

Manuel shook his head. "There was a fight because one of your girls resisted. Things got loud. Someone panicked. The crew split. The girls didn't make it back."

Taylor's hand tightened on the armrest. "Do you know where they are now?"

He exhaled. "No. Not yet."

Taylor cursed softly and stared out the window, the neon sign of another bar flickering in the distance.

"There's something else," Manuel said, his voice dipping.

She turned back toward him, bracing herself.

"They had a special interest in one of the women. Because she looks like someone important." He hesitated. "She looks a lot like the daughter of the ringleader. Same age too. A young woman who desperately wants to go to the U.S. but can't—because of her family's history."

Taylor's stomach dropped. "What kind of history?"

"Smuggling. Assault. A dozen flags on their record. Taking passports is a common thing among thieves here. They steal them from foreigners and use them to send people over the border."

"Has to be Gia. With her dark looks, she fits right in with the locals," Taylor said.

Sam's eyes widened. "So, they wanted her passport."

Taylor whispered, "That means they didn't just take her for a shakedown, then. They targeted her and got Madison with her."

Manuel nodded. "They're probably keeping the girls until the daughter can use Gia's documents to cross. It's all about timing. Getting someone over before the passport is flagged as stolen."

"Which means we're on a clock," Taylor said.

"Exactly," Manuel said quietly. "This is an unusual situation, and I hate to say this, but, considering the clout this family has, they might want to make sure there's no loose ends left behind."

Taylor's breath caught. Her gut twisted—

She pulled out her phone and typed furiously:

We have a lead. It's about the passport. I'll explain in person.

Keep everyone in the war room.

Sam looked up. "Then what's next?"

Manuel shifted the van into gear. "He didn't know where the girls are being held. But he gave me something—a name.

Someone who might. We find them. We press them." He looked at Taylor in the mirror. "We go fast. Before word gets around that we're out looking. How much money do you have on you?"

"Take us to an ATM," Sam said.

And just like that, the van pulled away from the curb, back into the night, chasing shadows.

Chapter Fourteen

Lucy drove south with her mind spinning, the tires humming a steady rhythm beneath her. At first, she'd had no destination in mind, just a vague sense that maybe Texas would be far enough—for now. The paranoia clung to her like smoke, every passing car a potential threat, every set of headlights a warning. Her grip on the wheel tightened as she glanced in the rearview mirror, half-expecting to see someone tailing her.

"Get it together," she muttered, her voice sharp and unforgiving.

Ginger twitched and tilted her head, questioning.

"No, not you, girl. I'm talking to myself." But the words did little to quiet the storm inside her.

She thought about Hart's Ridge, about the life she'd built there with her family. It seemed so distant now, like a dream she'd barely had time to grasp before it slipped through her fingers. She'd finally had a career too. Helping Faire Tinsley had been one of the few things that made her feel useful, and given her pride in herself. She'd brought Faire's talent to worldwide recognition again, the sales pouring in until they had more than enough. Enough for Lucy to start a business, to travel, to do whatever she wanted. She'd socked away every dollar she could, thinking soon she would be someone worth being. Someone her son could be proud of and maybe even someone who could find someone to love romantically, a man who would respect her and not treat her like dirt. Someone like Graham.

Oh, how Graham would've been head over heels with Johnny.

Her jaw clenched as her thoughts turned to her son. Her beautiful, sweet boy. He deserved so much better. Better than a mother who had done the things she'd done, who carried the kind of guilt she carried. She'd almost let someone take him for money. The memory of New York and Ian made her stomach churn, her grip on the wheel tightening until her knuckles turned white. Suki and her strange relationship with her brother, Ian, who was eager to be Johnny's father.

For a moment—a horrible, fleeting set of moments—Lucy had agreed and had nearly sold her soul for the promise of freedom and cash.

That was something she could never forgive herself for. Suki was still out there, and the question of what she would or could ever do to Lucy was a constant shadow bearing down on her, reminding her constantly of what she'd done.

What if Ian's father, the tough Ukrainian, was after her? Maybe the whole family was watching her, waiting for just the right moment to exact revenge.

What if Suki blamed Lucy for Ian's death? Pinning her own crime on the next best suspect? It had gone down on record as a home invasion and murder, but Lucy knew the truth. So did Suki, and, if her father had become suspicious, Suki would have no qualms about throwing Lucy under the bus to save her own ass.

A semi-truck came up beside her in the right lane and the

driver blew his horn, then leered at her and gave her a thumbs up. Waggling his eyebrows.

The blare of the horn made Ginger tremble, and Lucy flipped the driver off.

He scowled, making her chuckle through her tears. "God, you're such a mess," she whispered, blinking the tears away, refusing to let herself break down.

Not while she still had to keep moving.

She reached over and ran her hand through Ginger's hair, searching for comfort.

By the time she reached Fort Worth, the Jeep was running low on gas, and so was she. She pulled into a truck station on the outskirts of the city, its bright lights a harsh contrast to the dark stretch of highway she'd been traveling. The gas pumps were mostly empty, the quiet hum of machinery filling the air.

Lucy parked and stepped out, the cool night air biting at her skin as she filled the tank. Ginger stayed curled up in the passenger seat, her ears twitching at every sound.

Once the tank was full, she took Ginger on a short walk around the grassy area, put her back in the Jeep, then made her way to the station's diner. The place was nearly empty, just a few truckers scattered across the booths and at the counter.

She slid onto a stool at the far end of the counter, keeping her head down as she ordered a coffee and a plate of scrambled eggs and toast. The waitress brought the food without a word, and Lucy ate mechanically, her thoughts swirling.

She was halfway through her meal when a man sat down beside her. He was in his late forties, with a scruffy beard and a baseball cap pulled low over his forehead. His plaid shirt smelled faintly of diesel and sweat.

"Long night?" he asked, his voice gruff but not unkind.

Lucy didn't look up. "Something like that."

He didn't take the hint. "Where you headed?"

"Nowhere," she said shortly, taking a sip of her coffee.

The man chuckled, a low, gravelly sound. "Funny, that's where I'm headed too. Maybe we could keep each other company."

Lucy's stomach tightened. She kept her eyes on her plate, willing him to go away, but he leaned closer, his voice dropping. "I've got some cash. Enough to make it worth your while. What do you say?"

The words hit her like a slap. For a moment, she couldn't move, couldn't breathe. Her mind raced with the implications, the realization that he thought she was ... that kind of woman. And why wouldn't he? She'd been stupid to think she could ever shed who she used to be, to think she could outrun her past and all the bad things she'd done in her life.

Her hand trembled as she pulled out her wallet and slapped a few bills on the counter in front of the server. "Keep the change," she muttered, her voice flat.

The man watched her as she stood and walked outside, his eyes following her every move. The night was still and dark, the quiet hum of the highway in the distance. Lucy stood by the Jeep, the chill of the air doing nothing to calm her nerves. She felt hollow, like a shell of herself, the shadows pressing in from all sides.

She hated being alone.

Behind her, she heard the door of the diner swing open. She didn't turn around. She already knew who it was. The trucker's boots crunched on the gravel as he approached, stopping a few feet away.

"You waiting for me?" he asked, his tone quieter now, almost cautious.

Lucy didn't answer. She stared into the darkness, the stillness of the night beckoning her like an old friend. The temptation to let herself fall back into it—to give up, to stop fighting—

was overwhelming. What did it matter, anyway? She wasn't good enough for Johnny. She wasn't good enough for anything.

The man stepped closer, his presence looming. "Come on," he said softly. "I'll make it worth your while."

Lucy turned, her face expressionless as she nodded. Together, they walked toward his truck, the silence between them as heavy as the night. Somewhere deep inside, a part of her screamed to stop, to run, that she was better than this, but she shoved it down into a corner of her mind that was far from reality. Then she shut the door on it and locked it down.

No thinking allowed. Just block all the feelings.

She'd always been good at that.

Chapter Fifteen

They moved steadily through the backstreets of Cabo, where the noise of downtown faded into quieter, shadowed neighborhoods. The city lights blurred behind them, replaced by flickering porch bulbs, chain-link fences, and the occasional rusted-out pickup parked beneath sagging palm trees.

Manuel gripped the wheel with one hand, guiding them through turns with quiet confidence. He hadn't said much since they'd left the alley behind, but Taylor could feel the shift in the air—something had changed. Something big.

The tension in the van was coiled tight.

Taylor leaned forward slightly. "Who are we seeing?"

Manuel glanced at her in the rearview mirror. "Her name is Dulce. No last name needed. She's connected to the family behind this. The cousin of the girl they're trying to smuggle across the border using the stolen passport. Dulce doesn't get her hands dirty, but she makes things happen. She covers the logistics."

"Does she know where the girls are being held?" Taylor asked.

"She might," Manuel said. "Or she might know who does. Either way, she's our best shot right now."

They hit a rough patch of road, and the van rattled briefly before the pavement smoothed again.

"Before we meet her," Manuel said, "Like I said—Dulce doesn't talk for free."

Taylor felt Sam shifting beside her, pulling out his wallet.

Taylor frowned. "How much?"

"Depends how scared she is."

Manuel slowed the van near a faded corner market with a glowing Cajero Automático sign flickering against the stucco wall. An ATM.

"We'll stop here," he said. "Get at least two hundred. Small bills if possible."

Sam jumped out and headed toward the ATM, shoulders tense. Taylor stayed in the van, watching every movement outside, the silence inside thick as a held breath.

"Do you trust this Dulce person?" she asked.

Manuel didn't answer right away. Then, "No. But I trust the fear in her. And right now, fear might work in our favor."

Taylor nodded. Her heart pounded harder than it had all night.

Sam returned a few minutes later with a small stack of pesos and handed it to Manuel, who took the bills and tucked them into his jacket. "This is good enough to get us in the door."

They drove in silence, the van slipping deeper into the city, past shuttered storefronts and dark alleyways.

"We're meeting her in twenty minutes," Manuel finally said. "But we won't walk in cold. We'll park, watch, assess. No assumptions."

Taylor stared out into the night. "Good. Let's set the trap before someone else sets it for us."

The van rolled to a stop beneath a dark, crumbling overpass.

Overgrown vines crawled up one of the concrete pillars, and an old mattress leaned against a wall nearby, half-charred from a long-forgotten fire. Manuel killed the engine and turned off the headlights, shrouding them in shadows.

"She lives four blocks from here," he said, voice low. "No point in driving closer. People around here don't like uninvited visitors, especially not in vehicles they don't recognize."

Taylor climbed out, the pavement warm beneath her sandals even now. Sam followed her, keeping close. The air was thick with the scent of diesel, rotting food, and sea salt carried from the docks.

Manuel led them on foot through the narrow streets. Laundry flapped overhead on sagging lines. Old men played dominos beneath bare bulbs. Stray dogs watched from doorways, unmoving. Children darted past with wide eyes, silent as ghosts.

This wasn't the Cabo of brochures. This was the other side.

They turned into a cracked alley lined with rusted metal gates and doorways secured with chains and mismatched locks. Finally, Manuel stopped in front of a pale pink building with chipped paint and an arched window that looked like it hadn't been cleaned in years.

"This is it," he said. "Let me go first."

He tapped the door with a rhythmic knock. One beat. Pause. Two more.

After a moment, the door opened just a sliver. Taylor caught a glimpse of a woman's wary eyes peering through the crack. Then it opened wider.

Dulce was younger than Taylor expected—early thirties, maybe. Petite, with thick dark hair pulled into a messy braid, oversized hoop earrings, and sharp kohl-lined eyes that didn't miss a thing.

"You brought gringos to my home," she said to Manuel, unimpressed. *"Estás loco."*

"I brought people who need answers," he replied dryly.

Dulce looked Taylor over. "You police?"

"Used to be," Taylor answered. "Now I'm just someone who wants two innocent women to be brought home alive."

Dulce smirked faintly, then opened the door wider. "Then you'd better come in quick. And bring cash. My memory improves with pesos."

Taylor exchanged a glance with Sam, then stepped over the threshold, bracing herself for what came next.

Chapter Sixteen

The inside of Dulce's home smelled faintly of fried onions and damp laundry. A single bare bulb hung from the ceiling, casting weak light over a cramped living room cluttered with secondhand furniture and worn throw pillows. The walls were painted a faded mint green, streaked with fingerprints and peeling in the corners. The air was thick—not just with humidity, but with mistrust.

Taylor stepped inside cautiously, her eyes adjusting. She noted the heavy chain lock on the inside of the door, the second deadbolt, and the long wooden rod leaning beside it—an improvised weapon, likely used more than once.

Sam entered behind her, remaining close, shoulders taut. Manuel stayed near the door, his posture relaxed but watchful, like someone who knew better than to ever be fully at ease in a place like this.

Dulce walked ahead of them, barefoot, her anklet jingling softly with each step. "Sit," she said, gesturing to a sagging sofa that dipped in the middle.

Taylor perched on the edge, staying alert. This wasn't a social visit.

"I know why you're here already," Dulce said, dropping into an armchair across from them. She reached for a plastic cup on the end table and took a slow sip of something murky. "You want to know where the two girls are."

"We want to bring them home," Taylor corrected. Her voice was steady, her hands anything but. "Before they're used and discarded."

Dulce raised an eyebrow, unimpressed. "You make it sound so dramatic."

"Tell me I'm wrong."

A beat of silence passed. Then came the sound of movement behind the curtain that divided the hallway from the room—a rustle of cloth, a hush of bare feet. A tiny figure appeared: a little girl, no older than five, peeking out with wide, frightened brown eyes, clinging to the edge of the fabric.

Taylor's breath hitched.

Dulce glanced behind her shoulder. "Mija. Vete."

Without a word, the child disappeared again.

In that fleeting glimpse, Taylor saw it all. Hunger. Fear. The invisible weight of instability. The kind of childhood where every noise might be danger, and every adult might be the one who doesn't come home.

Sam leaned forward, his voice softer now. "We're not here to get you in trouble, Dulce. We're here to help our friends. And maybe help you too."

"Help me?" she echoed, her laugh bitter. "You think anyone can help someone like me?"

Her eyes flashed with something sharp. Not defiance—survival.

"You think I want to be mixed up in this?" she continued. "You think I had choices? I got a daughter back there who thinks the electricity turning off is just a game. I've skipped meals for her. Slept with a knife under my pillow. Prayed that the worst knocks would pass us by."

Taylor said nothing. She didn't need to. The silence spoke for her.

Manuel pulled a wad of pesos from his pocket and set it on the coffee table. "We're offering payment for information. Not judgment."

Dulce stared at the cash like it might burn her fingers.

"We know they targeted one of the girls," Taylor said. "Gia. Because she looks like someone. And she has a passport. You know about that, don't you?"

Lighting a cigarette she pulled from inside her shirt, Dulce took a shaky drag, her hand trembling now.

"I don't know exactly where they're being kept," she said at last. "But I know who you need to talk to. Her name's Yenni. She's the one who wants to cross. They promised her Gia's papers, but now she's scared. Because Gia's not cooperating. And the other one? The bride? She's loud. She's not letting it go quiet."

Taylor's throat tightened. "So, they're alive."

"For now," Dulce said flatly. "But if Yenni crosses and there's any blowback, they'll make sure the girls are nothing but whispers. You understand?"

Sam gathered the pesos from the table, sliding it across to Dulce. "Tell us where they are, and we'll bring more money. Dollars. Cash."

"I said I don't know exactly where," Dulce snapped. Her voice cracked.

"Another five hundred dollars if you find out," Taylor said calmly. "We'll go back to the machine and bring it back. We'll exchange the money for the location."

Dulce looked toward the curtain again, where her daughter had disappeared.

"You think I'm a monster," she said quietly. "But I've done what I had to do. So will Yenni. So would you."

She turned to Manuel, her voice resigned. "Go get the money. I'll give you what I know. But after this? You never saw me. You never heard my name."

"Deal," Taylor said, standing. Her voice didn't waver. "But when this is over, I hope that you separate yourself from people who will just yank an innocent person off the street and play with their life. I hope that little girl of yours grows up in a different kind of world."

Dulce didn't respond. She just lit another cigarette and stared at the flame.

Chapter Seventeen

Fort Worth was proving to be just what Lucy needed. Busy, loud, and so many people that she blended right in and felt comfortable enough to stay on a few days. She pushed the mop back and forth across the tile floor, the rhythm of her movements a hypnotic dance. The faint scent of bleach hung in the air, mingling with the musty scent of old wood and the faint tang of cooking spices wafting in from the common area. The hum of conversation drifted through the hostel's thin walls, mostly Spanish, fast and flowing, leaving Lucy to piece together only the occasional word. It didn't bother her. She didn't want to understand.

Keeping a low profile was her only priority.

Dyla's Hostel was everything she needed at the moment—small, clean, and close to the bus station in case she needed to make a quick getaway. The building's art-deco touches, with its gilded edges and geometric designs, might've once been grand, but now it was worn down, a shadow of its former self. Like her. Fitting. Lucy had splurged for a private room after being offered a half rate as pay. It wasn't much, but it was enough. Her room was windowless except for a vented opening facing the dimly lit hall, which suited her just fine. No need for sunlight or visibility. She wasn't here to be seen.

Ginger was allowed to hang out in the common area, and Lucy checked in on her often, making sure she had enough outside potty breaks. She seemed content and was a big hit with other guests too. Seemed everyone could use the comfort of a chill dog like Ginger.

Lucy had blisters from the mop, but she didn't mind. They made her feel useful, a visual and visceral reminder that she was doing something productive.

She leaned on the mop handle for a moment, her mind drifting. Nights were the hardest. She spent her evenings at nearby bars, nursing cheap beers and listening to the music bleeding through their cracked walls.

At times entertaining a free drink or two from some dumb sucker.

By the time she stumbled back to Dyla's, the streets would be eerily quiet, the downtown edges only shadowy alleys and flickering neon. The hostel locked up at midnight, but she always made it back just in time, her internal clock wound tight with the worry of being left to stay outside all night.

The trucker had been a huge mistake, and she wasn't doing that again. Nothing too unsavory had happened, but her reluctance had almost earned her a beating. She'd thought she could do it, just dissolve back into the girl she used to be, using sex as a weapon and a way to line her pockets a bit more. But faced with the opportunity, she'd found her heart wasn't in it. Or maybe that was the problem, her heart was in it now. It had known a different kind of life and, if she had let that man enter her and fill her with his wicked seed, she knew she would've vomited all over him.

Cleaning shitty toilets and oily floors was more appealing.

She got back to work, and the mop squeaked as she dragged

it over the tiles again, her focus snapping back to the present when a commotion broke out in the common area. Raised voices —one sharp and demanding, the other defensive—echoed off the walls.

"Not again," Lucy muttered, leaning the mop against the corner and stepping cautiously toward the source of the argument.

Dyla, the owner of the hostel, stood near the small reception desk, her arms crossed, her face set in a mask of calm authority that Lucy had come to admire. Dyla was a petite Mexican woman, but with a personality to be reckoned with. Considering the wide range of personalities that frequented the hostel, her fiery ways made it clear she wasn't to be messed with.

A broad-shouldered man stood inches from her, his gestures sharp and aggressive. Even without understanding his rapid Spanish, Lucy could see the tension in his body language. He was angry. She couldn't tell if it was about money, a complaint, or something else entirely, but he was leaning in too close, his voice rising.

"Basta!" Dyla snapped, her tone firm, but the man didn't back down.

Lucy stepped forward before she could think twice, her voice cutting through the tension like a blade. "Hey, back off."

Both Dyla and the man turned to her, startled. Lucy met the man's eyes, her expression hard. She wasn't in the mood for this. The man glared at her, his lips pressed into a thin line, but, after a tense moment, he muttered something under his breath and stomped toward the door, slamming it behind him.

Dyla exhaled sharply, a hand on her hip as she shook her head. "That guy has been trouble since day one," she muttered, switching to English. "Thanks for stepping in."

Lucy shrugged. "Figured you had it handled, but"—she gestured toward the door—"he was getting in your space."

Dyla's lips curved into a small smile. "I coulda handled him but you've got guts, chica. I like that." She paused, then nodded toward the stairs. "Come on. Let's get a drink. My treat."

Lucy hesitated, glancing at the mop in the corner. "I should probably—"

"It'll wait," Dyla interrupted, already heading for the staircase. "Come on."

With a resigned sigh, Lucy followed her upstairs to Dyla's room. The second the door opened, Lucy blinked in surprise. The room was a stark contrast to the rest of the clinically clean hostel. It felt warm and inviting, draped in deep reds and purples. It was a small studio layout with a tiny living area, kitchenette, and a corner dedicated to sleeping. Silken pillows were piled on the bed, and a tasseled lamp added soft glow across the space. It smelled faintly of jasmine and incense, the air heavy with an almost hypnotic comfort.

"Nice place," Lucy murmured, stepping inside.

"Thanks," Dyla said, grabbing two small glasses and pouring something amber colored from a decanter on the nightstand. She handed one to Lucy and flopped onto the bed, gesturing for Lucy to take the chair by the small desk. "You're a tough one to figure out, you know that? So quiet. So mysterious."

Lucy smirked faintly, taking a cautious sip of the drink. "Not much to figure out."

"Bull," Dyla said with a laugh. "Everyone's got a story." She studied Lucy for a moment, her expression softening. "You don't have to tell me though. I'm just glad you're not one of the crazies."

Lucy raised an eyebrow. "Is that the only bar we need to meet around here? Just under the crazy category?"

"You'd be surprised," she said, leaning back on her pillows, then pulling a small pouch out from beneath one. There was a pause before she added, almost casually, "So. You want to meet up with El Gata Diablo?"

"No thanks," Lucy said quickly. She didn't speak Spanish, but she knew some of the street slang and, yes, she'd fallen, but not far enough to get back on the stuff.

At least, not yet.

Dyla nodded slowly and slipped the pouch back under the pillow. "No worries. I respect that. So ... no boyfriend waiting for you somewhere? No girlfriend?"

Lucy's stomach tightened, but she kept her expression neutral. "No."

"Hmm." Dyla's eyes sparkled with mischief and flirtation. "Shame. You're pretty. You could have someone if you wanted. Someone like me, even."

Lucy gave her a polite smile and took another sip of her drink, wincing at the burn that trailed down her throat. Having someone meant getting to know them. Curiosity. Too many questions. Then complications. "I'm not looking."

Dyla laughed, shaking her head. "You're a tough one. I like that too." She tilted her head. "So, who broke your heart? Or did you break theirs?"

Lucy hesitated, her mind drifting to the series of men she'd held feelings for. First for Johnny's sperm donor, Maxwell Row. For a hot minute, she'd thought she loved him, but she was young and stupid. But Jorge Vanzo, her romantic artist from Uruguay, he was different. He'd treated her like she was somebody—he just didn't realize it was all an act. Ian had created Lucia, the elite art professional, and that's who Jorge had fallen for, not broken Lucy Gray from the foul chicken-farmed fields of Georgia.

Then her mind drifted to Graham. She thought about his easy smile, the way he didn't push, the way he'd made her feel—normal, almost. She could've loved him, given some time.

"There was someone," she admitted, her voice soft. She spun a story, weaving bits of truth and fantasy, blending both Jorge and Graham together in her mind. "He was ... different. Quiet, kind. Took me places, showed me things I'd never really paid attention to before."

Dyla leaned forward, intrigued. "And?"

Lucy's smile faded. She set her glass down, her fingers twisting together. "And nothing. I left."

"Why?" Dyla's tone was gentle, but her curiosity was sharp.

Lucy thought about the photo album. The Russian Museum with Graham and his wife posing proudly. What was Dyla trying to get at? And why all the questions when she'd not been interested before? She stared back at Dyla, trying to gauge what she was really thinking behind those long eyelashes.

"Are you okay?" Dyla asked, her brow suddenly wrinkled with worry.

Why would she worry about someone she didn't know?

Lucy stood abruptly, brushing her hands on her jeans. "I have work to finish," she said, her voice clipped. "Thanks for the drink."

Dyla watched her for a moment before sighing and nodding. "Suit yourself, chica."

Lucy left the room, her chest tight. She didn't look back.

It was time to leave again.

Chapter Eighteen

The small conference room inside the resort had transformed into a command post. They'd shoved aside the fancy coffee setup and resort brochures and replaced them with handwritten notes and a laptop that buzzed with quiet urgency. Thankfully, Heidi hadn't returned yet from her own investigation around the resort. That left only Cate and Ellis, Taylor and Sam, Brady—and Ryan, from the consulate.

"I haven't been given clearance to work this case," he said softly, looking at the closed door. "But I'm doing this off the record. Is that clear?"

They all nodded, grateful for his reluctant presence, especially since it meant their own country was standing by and doing nothing.

Taylor stood at the head of the table, leaning over the laptop. A pixelated satellite image filled the screen, the map zoomed in on a remote pocket of inland Cabo.

"There," she said, tapping the screen with a capped pen. "That's the compound Dulce described. An old ranch—weathered stucco, tin roofing. Looks abandoned from the air, but it's not. There's a perimeter wall, maybe six feet high, and what looks like an outbuilding behind the main house. Probably a stable or holding shed."

Sam hovered beside her, arms crossed. "Only one way in. This road here, dirt and narrow. No back exit. If we approach too fast or too loud, they'll see us coming long before we're close."

Ryan leaned in, his face grim. "And if we involve the local police now," he said, "they'll get tipped off before you even get there. I've seen it happen. Someone in the department makes a quiet call, and the people you're after vanish before you hit the front gate."

Cate let out a shaky breath. "So what do we do?"

Ellis sat beside her, eyes focused, fingers laced in front of him.

Brady stood near the window, facing away from the group, shoulders tight. He'd been quiet, simmering just below the surface. But now, he snapped.

"We go now," he said, spinning around. His eyes were bloodshot, his voice hoarse. "I don't care what maps say or who gets tipped off. We get in a damn car and we go. I will not sit here and wait while someone decides my wife's fate."

"Manuel's out there, waiting to pull up when we're ready," Sam said. "He can't let the staff here know he's helping us."

"Then let's go," Brady said again, his eyes wild.

Taylor opened her mouth to speak, but Ellis was already rising to his feet.

He walked slowly to Brady, placed a steady hand on his shoulder. His voice was low but carried weight.

"Son," Ellis said, "I know you're ready to break down that door. I feel the same. But if we go in hot—guns blazing—we don't just risk ourselves. We risk them."

Brady's jaw trembled. "She's my wife, Ellis."

"I know," Ellis said softly. "And she's my daughter."

The room was still.

Ryan stepped forward. "Listen, I've been through this before. You call in the cops too early, you lose your element of surprise. And that means losing the girls. So that means we wait until the moment we're inside. Then I'll call my liaison. We'll lock things down after they're safe."

Taylor nodded. "I like that. We go at night. Quietly. Park a few kilometers out, then approach on foot. Manuel's already working a contact to find out how many men are on the property. Once we confirm that, we move."

Sam added, "Right. Let's get our ducks in a row first. This isn't just about showing up. It's about getting out—with them."

Brady finally sank into a chair, resting his head in his hands. His fingers curled tightly, knuckles white.

Cate reached over, placing a hand gently on his back.

Taylor clicked her laptop shut. "We rest in shifts. Final plan goes into motion at midnight. Get food. Water. Anything you need. And prep quietly. I'll go speak to Rafael and tell him we're still looking and waiting on a call to come in from them. Let him think he's following the correct steps. We sure don't need any resort staff getting curious."

Chapter Nineteen

The black shirts were stiff and smelled faintly of plastic and starch, the kind of tactical gear that looked official but hadn't been worn enough to feel lived in. In addition to the clothes, Ryan had brought a small duffel bag of supplies—four two-way radios with earpieces, flashlights with red filters, zip ties, a pair of binoculars, and a thin roll of duct tape that Taylor didn't ask too many questions about.

He looked filled with nervous energy, and she would bet that something like this was what he dreamed of when he was sitting at the consulate every day, issuing visas and tracking down lost passports.

They gathered at the edge of the resort's property just after midnight, away from the glow of the lobby and far from any cameras. The air was thick and unmoving, pressed down by the weight of the approaching hour.

Taylor adjusted the earpiece over her right ear and tugged the shirt over her tank top. It hung a little long on her, but the fabric was breathable, and it blended well enough in the shadows. Still, it was hard to feel serious about a mission like this when you were wearing strappy sandals.

"They're the only shoes I brought that didn't scream 'wedding guest,'" she muttered, looking down at her feet. The soft leather rubbed her heel every time she shifted.

"You'll be fine," Sam said, handing her a flashlight. "You've done more with less."

"Yeah, but never on foot, in the desert, at night," she whispered back.

Ellis and Brady were a few feet away, checking the radios. Ellis was calm and composed—his years in the operating room lending him a surgeon's sense of control. Brady, on the other hand, looked like a man on the edge of combustion. His jaw was locked tight, his hands clenching and unclenching at his sides. They'd tried to talk him into staying behind in the war room, but he'd rejected their idea quickly.

Ryan stood with them, sleeves rolled, his tie long gone and his diplomatic demeanor replaced with quiet urgency.

The SUV Ryan had secured was parked down a long dirt lane outside the back gate of the resort, where no one from staff would see them depart. It was a beat-up white Suburban with sand-blasted paint and Mexican plates. No logos, no flash.

Just the way they needed it.

Taylor jogged awkwardly after the others as they moved out. The sandals slapped against the dust and grit of the road, and she immediately regretted not stuffing a pair of sneakers into her suitcase, regardless of how impractical it had seemed at the time.

They piled into the SUV, Ryan at the wheel, Sam beside him. Taylor sat in the middle row between Ellis and Brady. No one spoke much as they drove, the only sound the rattle of loose gear in the back and the soft chirps of insects outside.

About twenty minutes into the drive, Ryan finally broke the silence.

"Manuel's gone," he said, without turning around.

"What do you mean gone?" Sam asked.

"Gone as in he pulled out. Said he had a family to protect. And frankly ..." Ryan paused. "I don't blame him."

Taylor felt a sting of disappointment but couldn't muster anger. "He was never supposed to come this far," she said quietly. "He's right to protect what's his."

"Which leaves us," Ellis added, "with no local backup. No inside help. Just us."

"And no margin for error," Ryan said flatly.

They reached the drop point just before one a.m., pulling off onto a narrow strip of dirt that curved into a dry ravine. Ryan killed the headlights a quarter mile from the last marker, letting the vehicle roll to a quiet stop. They disembarked in silence.

The ranch was still a half-mile trek by foot.

The air smelled of dust and faint livestock. Somewhere in the distance, a coyote howled. The stars overhead were bright—too bright. Taylor wanted cloud cover. She wanted shadows.

Instead, they were walking into an open night with every movement exposed.

She squatted briefly to double-check her earpiece and the small radio clipped to her waistband. "We keep comms short. Just whisper. Don't say names. Stay in visual line when possible."

Brady nodded, but Taylor didn't miss the restless shift in his eyes. He was barely holding it together.

They moved single file through the scrub. The terrain was uneven, with rocks and twisted roots, and Taylor's sandals gave her no traction. Every few steps she stumbled, and more than once Sam reached back instinctively to steady her. She hated the sound her shoes made, the slap and scuff against the dry earth.

As they reached the crest of a shallow hill, Ryan crouched and held up a hand. Everyone dropped low beside him.

"There," he whispered, lifting the binoculars and pointing across the shallow valley.

Below them sat the compound. Just like in the satellite photo. Low buildings clustered behind a wall, the entire thing surrounded by a patch of dead trees and thorn bushes. There were no streetlights. No fences. Just the wall, maybe six feet high, with barbed wire laced along the top like a crown of rusted thorns.

One window in the main house glowed faintly yellow. A single porch light was on. No visible guards, no vehicles parked outside, but that didn't mean it was empty.

Taylor felt her stomach twist. The silence was deceptive.

Ryan passed the binoculars to Ellis. "If Yenni is here, she'll be inside the main building. Based on Dulce's description, the girls would be in one of the storage rooms behind it. If they're still here."

Taylor swallowed hard.

"If they've been relocated ..." Ryan didn't finish the sentence.

Taylor didn't need him to.

They crouched in the brush, watching, waiting. Listening.

Nothing moved. No dogs. No guards. Just the hum of desert insects and the ticking in her chest.

Then a light flickered on in the back building.

And a shadow passed across the window.

Someone was inside.

"Time to make our move," Taylor whispered.

But, as they stood, a far-off engine growled from the other side of the property.

Headlights flashed briefly through the trees.

Another vehicle was approaching.

And now everything was about to change.

Chapter Twenty

Once again, the highway stretched long and endless, dark but for the occasional glow of taillights cutting through the distance. Lucy had driven until exhaustion blurred the edges of her vision and her hands were stiff from gripping the wheel too tightly. Somewhere off the highway in Tennessee, she'd pulled into a rest stop, one of those deserted places meant for people just like her—too tired to drive, unwilling to pay or offer the identification needed for a hotel.

Her money was low too. Instead of a soft bed in a room she could afford if she had only brought her credit cards along, she parked at the far end of the lot, away from the flickering streetlamps and the big rigs lined up like sleeping giants. Now, curled up in the driver's seat with Ginger snoring softly in the back, she tried to sleep. But it wouldn't come.

No matter how she shifted, how she adjusted the seat, nothing felt right. The leather stuck to her skin, the air was thick, and her thoughts—God, her thoughts—were relentless. They ran in circles, past and present colliding until she didn't know which memories were real and which were just ghosts.

Her fingers dug into her bag, searching. She knew what she

was looking for, had known since the moment she stopped. The small orange bottle was cool against her palm as she pulled it out, the pills inside rattling softly.

Lucy stared at them, her breath catching.

It would be so easy.

The thought slid into her mind like a whisper, quiet but insidious. One handful, and it would all be over. No more running. No more waiting for the past to catch up to her. No more missing Johnny with a hurt so deep it felt like it was rotting her from the inside out.

She'd need to put Ginger outside. Let her find someone else to take care of her.

Her fingers tightened around the bottle, the plastic biting into her palm.

Johnny.

She squeezed her eyes shut, pressing her forehead against the steering wheel. She thought of his tiny hand waving goodbye as Alice escorted him out of the cabin to go to Taylor's house that last day. How excited he had been, blissfully unaware that it was the last time he'd see or touch his mother. How she had watched him walk away, not knowing she wouldn't be there when he came home.

What had he thought? Was he old enough to feel the loss?

She gasped out a sob, the kind that came from a place so deep it couldn't be softened or reasoned away. Her shoulders shook, her breath uneven, jagged.

She missed him. Missed him with an ache that had a shape, a weight, a presence that clung to her like a sickness. It lived inside her bones, a constant, gnawing thing that whispered *you don't deserve him anyway.*

Ginger stirred in the back seat, whining softly as if she sensed Lucy's distress.

She ran a shaking hand through her hair, gripping the roots

like she could hold herself together if she just clenched hard enough.

And then, like a switch had been flipped, her mind reeled further back.

To another loss.

She could still see the fire, even though she hadn't been there to witness it. Could hear the sirens. Could see her older sisters' faces, pale with horror. The house—her mother—her baby brother—gone.

And her? She had been off with her father and sisters, fishing. Just another day, another distraction. She hadn't been there. She had left them, and they'd died.

Her sisters always thought she was too young to remember, but they were wrong.

She remembered everything.

She remembered how they stopped speaking of her mother after the fire. How the loss was so big that nobody dared poke at it for fear it would swallow them all whole. But Lucy had grieved in silence, curled up under blankets that no longer smelled like her mother, sitting at a new dinner table where her voice was absent, the charred remains of their home branded permanently inside her mind as she tried to understand how someone could just cease to exist.

She had needed her mother. God, how she had needed her.

And then—somehow, impossibly—her mother had come back.

But now, all she got to see was Lucy screwing up, over and over again.

Lucy let out a broken laugh, shaking her head as she looked down at the bottle still clutched in her hand. God must really have it out for her to have given her a life worthy of a Lifetime movie. What had she done to deserve so much heartache?

Was all of it self-induced? Could she be the blame for everything she'd been through?

She twisted the cap off the medication bottle, spilling a few of the pills into her palm.

No, she thought angrily. She had no control over the fire that took her mother and little brother out of her life. God couldn't pin that one on her.

The rest of it, maybe.

Probably.

The pills glowed pale in the dim light, small but powerful. One choice. That's all it would take. She had enough. Enough to not only numb the pain, but to end it.

And then she heard Taylor's voice.

These will help, Lucy. You just have to trust me.

Taylor. Her rock. The one person who had never given up on her, even when Lucy had done everything in her power to make her do so. Her big sister had got her through school. Had held her through withdrawals. Picked her up off bar floors. Bailed her out of jail. Had cleaned her wounds and covered for her when she was too far gone to function.

Taylor had taken on the mother's role and, no, it wasn't perfect, but it made things a lot less brutal. And her sister had never, not once, lied to her. Even when the truth was brutally painful. But she was wrong about the mental illness.

Lucy didn't think she was sick. She didn't have some condition like Taylor thought. She was just messed up. Broken beyond repair.

Wasn't she?

Her breath hitched.

She thought about the mice. The incessant scurrying in her cabin back in Hart's Ridge. How it had driven her mad, scratching at the edges of her sanity, making her feel like she was unraveling.

What if the mice hadn't been real?

The question sent a sharp stab of fear through her.

What if she was wrong? And Taylor was right?

Lucy exhaled shakily and looked down at the pills.

One choice.

Slowly, she lifted one to her lips, her hand trembling as she swallowed it dry.

Just one. Not the whole bottle.

One was a step in the right direction.

She wasn't sure what would come next. But, for the first time in a long time, she was willing to find out.

Chapter Twenty-One

The soft rumble of an engine rose from the far side of the property—low and steady—growing louder by the second.

Taylor froze mid-step, crouched just behind Ryan and Sam, her hands braced against a rough patch of earth that crumbled under her palms. She felt her heart leap up into her throat as two beams of light cut through the dark, slicing across the edge of the ranch's outer wall. The headlights bobbed with the uneven road, throwing harsh shadows that danced along the barbed wire fence.

"Shit," Sam muttered under his breath.

Ryan dropped into a low crawl and motioned them down. "Don't move. Don't silhouette." His voice crackled softly in the earpiece. "Everyone stay low."

Taylor flattened herself to the ground. The dirt was warm from the day's sun, but it carried a bitter metallic smell, like dried blood and diesel. The ridgeline they'd hidden behind now felt far too exposed. Her feet slid and she grabbed the ground, getting a cocklebur in her palm. She cursed her sandals, which made even her stillness feel conspicuous.

The vehicle—a dusty black pickup with a cracked taillight—creaked to a stop at the main gate. One man stepped out. His silhouette was long and lean, his stride casual in a way that made Taylor uneasy. He didn't knock. He didn't call out. He simply walked up and entered through a side door in the gate, disappearing into the darkness as if he belonged there.

"Late-night company," Ellis whispered, crouched beside her.

Ryan adjusted his radio. "That gate wasn't locked," he said. "He walked right in. Not standard behavior for a hostage scenario."

Taylor narrowed her eyes at the now-dark entrance. "Unless they're not afraid of anyone coming."

Sam leaned closer to her, his breath warm against her ear. "Do we wait?"

Taylor shook her head. "We watch. Time it. We need to know how many are inside. If that's Yenni, we might be able to tail her. If it's someone worse, we need to know what we're walking into."

They lay still, the minutes dragging.

A second light flicked on in the back building. The structure Dulce had called "the holding room."

Inside, two shadows moved—one tall, one shorter. Taylor focused on the smaller one, who pressed against the window bars like they were trying to see out.

Her chest tightened. Gia?

She reached for the binoculars, adjusted the focus. The image wobbled slightly, then cleared just enough to catch a flash of blonde hair on a figure behind the one pressed against the window.

It's got to be Madison, Taylor surmised. They were still there. Both still alive.

Taylor felt relief crack like ice inside her—but it didn't last.

Because, if they were still here, and that man had just arrived, the clock had started ticking again.

"Time to move?" Sam's voice whispered through the radio, impatient.

"Not yet," Taylor answered firmly. "Wait for the lights to go out. We don't know who just arrived or why."

She turned to Ryan. "We need to sweep the rear first. That stable—if it's empty, we use it to flank the house. Quiet entry. One window. One door. We control the space."

Ryan nodded. "We'll go silent from here. Five minutes."

Ellis adjusted his earpiece. "And if they see us?"

Taylor's voice was ice. "Then we improvise. But we're not leaving without those girls."

They crawled backward first, away from the ridgeline, then shifted to single-file movement, using the brush as cover as they made their way downhill.

The sand was loose and treacherous underfoot, and her sandals slid every few steps. Sam gave her an apologetic glance, as if he knew the next day her feet would be raw.

She didn't care. Not as long as they got to that room in time.

As they neared the back of the ranch wall, Taylor held up a hand. The outline of the stable came into view—no lights, no movement.

But the wind shifted, and suddenly the faintest whimper reached her ears.

Someone was crying.

Inside that stable.

She pointed to Sam and Ellis, gesturing for them to take the far corners. Brady flanked Ryan. Taylor crept to the door.

She pressed her ear to the wood.

And heard a voice.

Female.

Terrified.

"No ... please, don't ..."

Taylor's blood went cold.

She drew her flashlight slowly, clicked it to red mode, and nodded to Sam.

They were out of time.

Chapter Twenty-Two

The sound of the engine was gone now. The last flicker of headlights had vanished behind the rusted fence, swallowed by the darkness around the compound. But the silence that followed was far from peaceful. It pressed against Taylor's eardrums like rising water.

She crouched near the rear of the stable, one hand hovering just above the wooden door latch, her other planted against the rough grain of the planks. The door was warped and cracked near the bottom, the scent of rot and ammonia drifting through the seams.

A whisper buzzed through her earpiece: "Clear up front. One man still on the porch," Sam said. "No other movement. Proceed when ready."

Taylor drew in a breath. The moment had arrived. No turning back.

She gave the hand signal—ready, flank left, flank right—then mouthed a silent three-count to the others.

One ... two ...

On three, she eased the latch upward. The mechanism

groaned louder than she'd expected, and she flinched. Sam stepped in beside her, flashlight pointed toward the floor.

They moved in.

The air hit her like a slap. Thick and warm, pungent with mildew, unwashed hay, old urine, and fear. Her red-filtered flashlight cut through the dark in a wide arc. Dust danced in the beam like ash.

In the far corner of the stable were two figures—one standing protectively in front of the other.

The shorter woman stepped forward, eyes flashing with distrust and something deeper: relief.

"Gia?" Taylor asked softly.

Gia's mouth trembled. "Who are you?"

"I'm Taylor, Ellis' stepdaughter. He's with me."

The second she spoke, the tension snapped. Gia stumbled forward and crashed into Taylor's arms. Her thin frame trembled against her, ribs rising and falling too fast. "I didn't think you were real," she whispered. "I thought it was another trick."

Taylor hugged her tighter. "No trick. We've got you."

Behind her, Madison slowly pulled herself upright. Her face was pale beneath a smudge of dried blood on her temple, her blonde hair matted and sticking to her cheek. But her voice was steel.

"Took you long enough."

Taylor turned toward her with a breathless smile. "Still got that fire, huh?"

"I've been telling them every day they picked the wrong bride to mess with," Madison said. "You get tired of threatening someone when they never stop talking back."

"They bound her wrists as punishment," Gia said.

Sam and Ellis moved through the adjacent stalls, checking corners and shadows with smooth precision.

"All clear," Sam called softly.

When Ellis came closer, Madison finally broke.

"Dad? Is that you?"

Ellis ran to her and knelt, taking her into his arms as he cried into her hair.

"Let's hold the reunion for later," Sam said. "We need to get you two out of here. How many are in the house?"

"Two. Yenni and her boyfriend," Gia said.

Ellis examined the zip ties binding Madison's wrists. The plastic had bit into her skin, leaving angry ridges.

"Hold still," he said gently. "You might have some abrasions."

"I've had worse hangovers," Madison muttered, but her voice cracked near the end. She glanced sideways at Gia, who had sunk to the floor against the stable wall, her arms wrapped tightly around her knees.

"We overheard them talking," Madison whispered now, softer, her bravado slipping. "Yenni wants out. She's scared. Said we weren't worth the risk anymore. She was going to move us tonight—before sunrise."

"Her boyfriend argued with her about it. Not sure who won," Gia added from the floor, her voice scratchy. "They were talking about the docks. A boat, maybe. We don't know for sure."

Taylor crouched in front of her. "You're safe now, but we don't have much time. One wrong move and they'll scatter—or worse. Do you think they're armed?"

"Yenni's boyfriend is," Madison said. "He's young ... tall, shaved head. He kept patting his hip. I think he's trigger happy."

"Got it," Taylor said. She turned and gave Sam a nod.

That was when the rear door opened, and Brady stepped into the stable, silhouetted by the moonlight. His eyes swept the room, then locked on Madison.

She moved first, launching herself into his arms with a sob that echoed off the rafters and made the rest of them cringe.

"Shh ..." Taylor hissed.

Brady didn't listen. He held her like a drowning man grabbing a lifeline, murmuring something only she could hear, his arms locked tightly around her as though to shield her from anything that might come next.

Taylor gave them just a moment before turning back to her radio.

"Ryan, status?"

A pause. Then: "Still one on the porch. He's distracted. Smoking again. We've got a two-minute window—maybe."

Sam whispered, "We can't take both girls through the front. They'll be seen. We need to retrace and move fast."

Taylor nodded, already moving toward Gia. "Can you walk?"

Gia nodded shakily. "Yes. Just help me up."

Taylor reached down, wrapped her arm around her, and pulled her to her feet. Gia stumbled, then steadied herself with Taylor's support.

Sam covered the exit, his hand on the flashlight and his eyes scanning constantly.

"Move now," Taylor ordered. "Back the way we came. Quiet. Stay low."

They filed out into the brush again, Gia between Taylor and Sam, Madison and Brady bringing up the rear.

They had taken barely ten steps when a door slammed open on the opposite side of the compound.

A porch light flared to life.

Voices. Two. Then three. Raised, sharp.

"Go!" Taylor hissed, urging Gia forward.

The still night had shattered.

They had been seen.

Chapter Twenty-Three

They were almost out. So close Taylor could taste the sea air—salty and dry, drifting on the wind like the promise of safety. Her feet ached, her legs shook, and her hands gripped Gia's arm so tightly it had become an extension of her own.

But when they rounded the last curve of the compound, the exit in sight, a figure emerged from the shadows.

"Whoa, whoa," the young man said, stepping forward with easy arrogance. "Party's not over yet."

He was wiry and lean, maybe twenty-five. A tattoo crept up the side of his neck like ivy, and he had the kind of smile that made Taylor's skin crawl—wide, smug, and too calm for the chaos unraveling around him.

Gia gasped and shrank back. "That's him. Rodrigo."

"The illiterate bastard," Madison said, the last word muffled as she was pulled down to the ground by Brady.

Taylor stepped in front of Gia protectively. "We're leaving. Get out of the way."

Rodrigo lifted both hands in mock surrender, still grinning.

"I don't think so. You just broke into my house, kidnapped my girls. Bit rude, no?"

"We're not asking," Sam growled.

Rodrigo's smile dropped. He reached slowly toward his waistband.

Taylor's heart seized. Weapon.

Before she could react, a voice rang out from behind them, sharp and firm.

"Hands where I can see them. Now."

Taylor whipped her head around. Ryan.

He was twenty feet back, gun drawn in a two-handed grip, stance steady, earpiece still tucked in. The barrel of the weapon pointed squarely at Rodrigo's chest.

Ryan has a gun? She felt heat crawl up her neck. Her jaw clenched. *All this time, I thought we were doing this clean. Unarmed. Controlled.*

She would have made different calls—wouldn't have brought the girls out into this standoff if she'd known the rules of engagement had shifted.

Rodrigo's eyes narrowed. "Oh, look. Someone has bite."

"You want to walk away from this?" Ryan's voice was cold steel. "Then don't reach again. I won't ask twice."

Tension coiled like a live wire between them. One wrong move and someone would be dead.

Then, a shout split the air.

"Stop it!"

A figure sprinted from the far side of the compound, barefoot and wild-haired, arms pumping at her sides. She looked so much like Gia.

It had to be Yenni.

She shoved past Sam and Taylor, inserting herself between Rodrigo and Ryan with reckless desperation. "What are you doing?" she screamed, spinning on Rodrigo first. "What the hell are you doing?"

"Get back," he barked, trying to grab her arm.

She jerked away. "No! You think I want this?"

"Yenni, not now," he hissed, glancing toward Ryan's pistol. "Your father said—"

Her voice cracked. "I don't care what he said. He told me it was just a shakedown for the passport! That no one would get hurt! That it would all be over in one night!"

Ryan didn't lower the gun.

"I'm not going to the U.S. with blood on my hands," Yenni cried, turning in a slow circle, pleading with all of them now. "Don't you get it? I want to leave because of this! Because I hate this life! The bribes, the threats, the fear—all this!"

Taylor stepped closer. This was the moment. "Then help us end it. Right here, Yenni. Right now."

Yenni's face crumpled. She reached slowly toward her ankle —Taylor tensed again—but, instead of a gun, she pulled a small knife free and held it out, blade-down.

She walked forward and dropped it in the dirt.

"I'm done, Rodrigo," she whispered. "Let these girls go. Let me go."

Rodrigo's mouth twisted. "You're making a mistake."

"No, my father made the mistake," Yenni snapped. "He thought I was just like him. I swear to you, I'll find my way out of this hellhole of a town, but it'll be on my own. Without either of you."

Taylor saw the shift then—the dangerous glint vanish from Rodrigo's eyes, replaced by something colder. Calculating.

"We're not out of this yet," Ryan said softly. "He's thinking through options."

Rodrigo shifted his weight. His hand inched back toward his waistband again.

Taylor reacted on instinct as she grabbed the knife from the dirt. She stepped forward, her voice commanding. She wielded it. "Don't even think about it."

"I'm not scared of you," Rodrigo said.

"Then you're a fool," Sam muttered.

Behind them, Ellis pulled Madison behind a crumbling wall. Brady stood in front of her, arms out like a human shield.

Gia trembled against Taylor's side.

Ryan spoke again. "This is over, Rodrigo. If you want to walk away breathing, turn around and go."

Rodrigo looked at Yenni, then at the gun still trained on his chest.

Something in his face changed. He stepped back once, twice. Then he spat into the dirt and turned around. "You'll regret this, Yenni."

She didn't reply.

Rodrigo disappeared into the shadows, and, for a long, tense beat, no one moved.

Taylor exhaled. Her arms were trembling.

She turned to Ryan. "You didn't tell me you were armed."

"I didn't think we'd need it," he replied. "Then everything changed."

Taylor glared at him. "Next time, tell me everything. I don't go in blind—not when lives are on the line."

Ryan gave a curt nod. "Fair enough."

Yenni still stood frozen in place, her chest heaving.

Taylor approached slowly. "We can help you, Yenni," she said. "You cooperate, you might just walk away free. But no more lies. No more games."

"Please help me. I'm done with all of it," Yenni whispered, her voice hollow. "I just want out. He's probably in there now, calling my father."

Taylor nodded. "Then let's move. Before someone else

shows up with a bigger gun and no conscience." She turned back to the others. "We move fast. Eyes everywhere."

And, with that, they disappeared into the brush once more—bruised, barefoot, shaken.

But not broken.

———

"Keep your heads down!" Taylor whispered harshly, gripping Gia's arm and practically dragging her up the small incline. Her legs burned, and the world narrowed to three things: the girls, the van, and the growing sense that they were being followed.

Madison stumbled again, and Brady nearly dropped to his knees catching her.

"Madison!" Ellis called out, alarmed.

"I've got her," Brady said, voice raw. "I've got you, Mads. Just hang on a little longer."

"Someone's behind us," Ellis hissed from the rear. "Movement. Can't confirm if it's them, but we're not alone."

Taylor's heart pounded so hard it echoed in her ears.

"Double time," Ryan ordered from the rear. "Forget stealth. Run."

And they did.

The dry scrub slapped at their legs as they broke into a sprint. Taylor's sandals barely held on—twice she kicked one sideways and had to correct mid-stride. Gia kept up, silent and gasping, her fingers still wrapped in Taylor's.

The SUV came into full view, moonlight casting silver across the hood.

"Go! Doors open!" Ryan barked, already hitting the fob. The vehicle beeped, lights flashing briefly.

Brady threw the rear door open and hoisted Madison inside.

Sam practically lifted Gia into the middle row. Taylor grabbed Ellis's elbow and shoved him in beside Ryan.

That left Yenni.

"Get in!" Taylor yelled.

The girl hesitated, turning around and looking toward the ranch.

And then Taylor heard it.

Engines.

Distant. Faint. But coming fast.

"It's my father's men," Yenni yelled. "They'll shoot to kill."

"Get in," Taylor snapped as she jerked Yenni's shirt, pulling her across her lap and barely getting her legs in before she slammed the passenger door. "Drive!"

Ryan gunned the engine and Yenni struggled to get up from where she'd landed on the floor.

The tires spit up gravel as the SUV shot forward, headlights off, taillights dimmed. They hit the road at a jolt, fishtailing slightly, then found traction.

Inside, everyone was panting, shaking, the adrenaline thick in the air like static.

"Did they see us?" Gia asked, her voice paper-thin.

"I don't think so," Ellis said, peering out the rear window.

"I know so," Taylor said, watching the mirror.

In the distance, headlights appeared.

Two vehicles. Fast.

Too fast.

"Hang on," Ryan said grimly. "This just got harder."

Chapter Twenty-Four

The SUV roared over the cracked earth, tires spitting dust into the night like a dragon's breath. Ryan gripped the wheel with both hands, his knuckles pale, jaw tight with focus. The headlights were off—by necessity, not strategy—but the moon offered just enough to see the undulating terrain stretching into nowhere.

Taylor glanced back. Two sets of headlights still chased them, bouncing in and out of dips in the road. No sirens, no horns—just the relentless growl of engines that were gaining.

"We're not going to outrun them," Ellis muttered from the back seat, checking his watch for the fifth time in ten minutes.

"We just need another mile," Ryan snapped. "There's a wash up ahead. We lose them in the rock bed, then double back."

But the van was rattling harder now. Taylor felt it in her bones. The uneven terrain wasn't just chewing the tires—it was grinding them to threads.

Then came the snap.
BOOM.
The back left corner dropped. The van fishtailed hard, skid-

ding sideways and jarring everyone in their seats. Madison screamed. Brady braced a hand on the ceiling.

"We lost a tire!" Sam shouted.

"I know!" Ryan slammed the brakes, the van groaning as it swerved sideways and rolled to a stop behind a sparse patch of scrub.

"Everyone out!" Taylor yelled. "Take cover!"

They spilled from the van, dragging Gia and Madison with them, moving fast and low. Sam led them to a dip in the landscape—a dry arroyo with just enough of a ridge to disappear behind. They slid down the embankment, dust kicking up as they crouched among rocks and brush.

Taylor counted them once. Twice. Everyone was there.

Then silence.

And then—

Engines cutting off.

Doors slamming.

Footsteps.

Taylor and Ryan locked eyes. They were sitting ducks. The others looked to her for a plan she didn't have. She turned to Ryan, her voice low. "Call your contact. We need backup. Now."

Ryan pulled his phone. "I'll send our coordinates."

Twenty still and tense minutes later, the headlights had gone dark, but their enemies hadn't left. No one moved. Not them, and not Taylor's team.

An hour passed. The desert cooled, the dry air carrying every creak of boots, every breath. Gia sat trembling between Taylor and Yenni, who had barely spoken since the standoff began.

"They're waiting for something," Sam whispered.

"No, they're waiting for someone," Taylor corrected.

And then he arrived.

The black SUV appeared like a phantom from the horizon—no lights, just the hum of its engine breaking the silence. It stopped a dozen yards from the ridge. The other men stepped aside without a word. Doors opened.

Yenni straightened beside Taylor. "It's him."

"Your father?" Taylor asked.

Yenni nodded.

The man who stepped out was in his late fifties, face lined by sun and hardship. He wore a crisp collared shirt, sleeves rolled, rosary beads swinging slightly at his wrist. When he moved, the others stepped back.

He lifted his hand and called out. "I want to speak to my daughter."

Taylor and Ryan exchanged a look.

"He won't hurt me," Yenni said.

"I'll allow it," Taylor said quietly. "But we stay between them and everyone else."

Ryan added, "No sudden moves. And stay ready."

Taylor stood slowly and led Yenni out from the arroyo, stepping carefully as they emerged into the moonlight. The men watching from a distance didn't interfere.

Yenni's father approached, slowly, like he was walking through fog. He approached his daughter and sighed, looking at her as though she were a small child.

"Yenni," he said. "What are you thinking? You've put us in grave danger."

"No. You put us in peril the second you took those girls," she replied.

He shook his head, face darkening. "It wasn't supposed to happen like that, and you know it, but that's neither here nor there right now. You think this is about two girls? This is about survival. You think the government up north cares about us? You think they make it easy for people like us to do things the right way?"

Taylor didn't speak. She let the moment be his—until it turned.

"You think I wanted your brother to rot in prison?" he barked, his tone suddenly harsh and angry. "You think I wanted your mother working three jobs just to feed you while I smuggled scrap metal in the dark? Should we go back to that? Should we not send you ahead for a good life? Daughter, think about this—our world doesn't give chances often. It takes them. Perhaps finding this girl, this Gia, was your destiny. Her life for yours. You want to give that opportunity up?"

Yenni's chin lifted. "I won't go. Not with that hanging over me. Not on the shadow of someone else's pain." She trembled, and more tears rolled down her face. She rubbed at them like a small child would. "I just wanted to be normal," she whimpered. "I wanted to live somewhere where we don't have to lie or run or hide. Where we don't hurt people to get ahead."

"It's not only about the passport now, Yenni," he said, lowering his voice again. "If we don't fix this mess you've made —we're all done for. They'll come for us. For your mother too. Your brother will suffer more than he already does. We both know the cartel won't take kindly to what we've done here. With how things have gotten out of control. You want even more blood on your hands? Your own family's blood?"

She didn't reply. Only stared stubbornly at him.

"We fix it, and no one is the wiser."

"I know how you fix things, *Papi*. None of these people will leave here breathing."

"Shut your mouth," he hissed and stepped closer. "You're a fool."

Closer still.

Taylor noticed his hand dip slightly, toward the small of his back.

"Back up," she said sharply. "Stay where you are."

"You think you understand this?" he sneered. "You Americans with your clean borders and clean laws. You've never had to watch your children starve. Never had to sell your soul just to keep them breathing."

"You're wrong," Taylor said. "And you've already sold yours."

He turned to Yenni.

"I gave you a chance," he growled. "And you're throwing it away. Now I clean it up."

Then—he drew.

Fast.

Taylor reached too late.

CRACK.

A single shot rang out.

Yenni gasped.

Her body jolted.

She staggered backward—and collapsed.

"No!" Taylor dropped to her knees, catching her just before she hit the ground.

Gia screamed.

The father stood frozen, arm trembling, gun still raised—until Ryan surged forward, weapon drawn.

"Drop it!" he bellowed.

Yenni looked up at her father as blood soaked through her shirt. Her lips quivered, her breath coming in short gasps.

"I see it now," she whispered. "A place ... better than America. It's so beautiful, Papá. Every little thing about it ..."

Her father stumbled forward, face broken. "*Mija ...*"

She smiled faintly and touched his cheek. "I forgive you, Papá"

Then her eyes closed.

Taylor reached for her pulse, felt it flutter once ... then go still.

Her father dropped the gun.

He fell to his knees, clutching his rosary beads. "I didn't mean to ... I didn't mean ... I wasn't aiming at ..." He let out a roar—an animalist cry of grief. When he stopped, he looked at Gia, at Taylor, at Ryan.

"Go. All of you. Just ... go." His head dropped again.

Taylor hesitated as she searched the horizon.

They weren't going anywhere yet.

He didn't lift his head.

He turned to his men and barked something in Spanish—sharp and final. They began dispersing, no arguments. Some bowed their heads. One wept. But they left in their vehicles, pulling out quickly, raising a dust tornado.

Taylor stood as police sirens echoed in the distance. Blue and red strobes blinked on the horizon, drawing closer. The father knelt beside his daughter, muttering prayers in Spanish.

Then he reached again—for his gun.

Taylor saw it.

"No!" she screamed.

Sam lunged forward, knocking the weapon away just before the shot.

"No way," Sam said, breathless with fury. "You don't get the easy way out. You have to live with this and tell her mother what you did."

He broke.

Collapsed.

Sobbing.

As the police descended, weapons raised and shouting, Taylor took one last look at Yenni's body—arms slack, a breeze lifting her hair. It was a damn shame. She turned away.

Because there was nothing left to save there.

Chapter Twenty-Five

The two-lane road curved through the hills like a lazy ribbon, the deep greens of West Virginia rolling past Lucy's window in the setting sun. The sky above was thick with low-hanging clouds, softening the sunlight into a pale haze that made everything look a little dreamlike. Lucy had been driving for hours, her only companion the steady hum of her tires and the soft snuffling of Ginger curled up in the passenger seat.

They'd have to stop soon. Lucy needed to relieve her bladder and her hunger, and her dog would need the same. The gas tank also begged to be filled.

She still wasn't entirely sure if the pill she'd taken the night before had done anything, or at least, much. Her mind felt sharper, less foggy at least, though there was still an edge of unease—like something just out of sight was waiting for her to let her guard down. Taylor had told her the meds would take the edge off, that they'd help her separate the truth from the stories her brain spun when it was in survival mode. But Lucy had lived in that mode for so long it was hard to tell where reality ended ... and paranoia began.

Your brain tells you lies, Taylor had said once, holding her hand while Lucy fought through a panic attack so bad she couldn't breathe. The trick is knowing which voice to listen to.

Lucy wasn't sure she'd ever learned that trick. Not yet. Not completely.

Ginger stirred as Lucy eased off the highway into a town so small it barely registered on the map. The sign at the entrance read Welcome to Sparrow's Hollow, Population 802. Just the kind of place Lucy had been sticking to lately—out-of-the-way, forgettable, where no one paid attention to strangers passing through.

She parked in a gravel lot next to a weathered wooden sign that pointed toward Devil's Eye Overlook—some local site, she guessed, that would give her an excuse to stretch her legs. Ginger's tail wagged the second Lucy reached for her leash, and they stepped out into the cool, damp air, the scent of rain clinging to everything.

The path to the overlook was short, winding through a patch of forest that led to a rocky outcropping. Below them, the valley stretched wide, fog drifting in delicate tendrils over a shallow river. The wind stirred Lucy's hair, and, for a moment, she could almost pretend she was just another tourist. A woman with her dog, out for a scenic walk.

The moment didn't last.

She bought a couple of hot dogs from a food cart near the overlook's parking lot, tearing off bits for Ginger before sitting on a weathered picnic table. The wood was damp, but she didn't care. The familiar weight of her paranoia settled at the edges of her mind, like a storm cloud that never completely drifted away.

She kept her back to the road, her eyes on the forest beyond, reassuring herself there were no black SUVs, no cameras flashing from the trees. Her brain whispered that there might be —that Ian's people might still be searching for her, or that

Every Little Thing

Graham, sweet, too-good Graham, had gone digging into who she really was after she disappeared.

But the pills were kicking in, she could feel it now—the faintest separation between herself and those racing thoughts. They felt like they belonged to someone else, someone just over her shoulder, instead of wrapping themselves around her throat.

Lucy, your brain lies ...

The photograph of Graham and his wife in front of the Russian museum taunted her. Was it simply a coincidence?

She exhaled slowly, her fingers threading through Ginger's fur as her mind drifted.

She could picture the farm in Hart's Ridge, the creak of the porch under her bare feet, the smell of hay drying in the sun. She imagined Johnny running through the tall grass, laughing, his arms stretched wide like an airplane. Johnny following behind the other kids, struggling to keep up but happy to be included. He deserved that kind of life—a childhood full of joy and safety, not the chaos and fear she'd been running from for so long.

She imagined herself there, too, standing by the fence, her hands resting on the weathered wood, her heart no longer constantly clenched in fear. Could she ever be that person? Could she go home and be someone her son could trust to always be there, without running, without hiding?

A painful lump formed in her throat at the thought. Maybe if she could just stop looking over her shoulder long enough to build something real.

Her gaze drifted to Ginger, staring up at her as she waited for another bite of the wiener. The dog had become more than a companion in these past weeks—she was a tether. A reminder that someone relied on her, even if it was just for food and a place to sleep.

Like Johnny had.

Lucy wanted to believe that could be enough. But the shadows always returned. The ghosts of who she'd been, what she'd done, the things she could never undo.

Her thoughts inevitably drifted to Johnny's real father. The man she had once convinced herself could be trusted, who had promised to stay away after she refused to let him into Johnny's life. His words had sounded convincing back then, but Lucy knew better now. Words meant nothing when someone was desperate enough.

And Maxwell had a lot of power.

So did Ian. Even from the grave.

She would protect Johnny at all costs now. Her fingers tightened around the paper wrapper from her hot dog, crumpling it into a tight ball. She knew where she was going. She couldn't admit it to herself out loud yet, but the pull had been there from the moment she left Graham's house.

Some shadows had to be confronted head-on.

But what then? What if she survived it—what if she came out the other side with no more demons chasing her? Could she build a life in Hart's Ridge? Not just for Johnny, but for herself?

She'd never really thought about it before. Not seriously.

The idea of love—real love, with someone kind and steady—had always felt like a fantasy she wasn't allowed to touch. But what if there was someone who could see all her jagged edges and still want to build something with her? Someone who could love Johnny like their own, who could help her give him the stability she'd never had.

The thought felt too fragile to hold onto, but it was there. A flicker of possibility in the storm of her mind.

She brushed her hands off on her jeans and stood, clipping Ginger's leash back on. It was time for her to take her medication. Pill number two—something she didn't want to do but was also now curious to see if it could help.

"Come on, girl," she murmured, her voice soft. "We've got a long way to go."

The dog wagged her tail and trotted beside her, oblivious to the storm inside Lucy's chest and their next stretch of highway.

The road called to her again, stretching out into the darkness. One step closer to a confrontation she couldn't avoid. One step closer to whatever life she might be brave enough to build after it was all said and done.

Chapter Twenty-Six

The war room didn't feel like a war room anymore. It felt like the backroom of a police station—the air thick with tension, the lingering smell of stale coffee and unspoken questions curling like smoke.

Taylor sat at the far end of the long table, arms crossed tightly over her chest. Her shoulders ached. Her feet throbbed. Her sandals—mud-caked and cracked—sat discarded near the door. She hadn't spoken more than a dozen words since they returned from the desert at dawn. Exhaustion had settled deep into her bones.

Now it was morning, and the room buzzed with movement.

Bridesmaids with smudged mascara whispered in corners. Groomsmen hovered awkwardly, unsure whether they should be cracking jokes or offering hugs. One of them—barefoot and still drunk—held a mimosa like a life raft, eyes wide with the shell shock of realizing his vacation had turned into a headline.

Hazard and Anna sat curled together on a love seat against the wall, legs tangled like teenagers, heads leaned together. She laughed at something he whispered—too softly, too soon.

Taylor tried not to judge. They'd all been through hell.

Across the table, Madison sat upright, pale and composed, though her fingers gripped a pen with such tension it looked like it might snap. Gia sat beside her, shoulders hunched, eyes swollen but sharp. Harder than they had been before.

Two uniformed officers from the local Cabo precinct sat in metal chairs opposite the girls, nodding blandly as they scribbled in notepads they didn't seem to be reading. Their badges gleamed. Their expressions didn't.

"Can you tell us again what happened after you left the private pool?" one of the officers asked in heavily accented English, his voice void of emotion.

Gia exchanged a glance with Madison. "We already told you. Three times."

"And we provided written statements," Madison added, her voice clipped but calm. "And video."

"Yes, yes," the other officer said, waving his hand as if swatting a fly. "But this is ... routine. For records."

Taylor watched the exchange with a tightening jaw.

Routine.

A girl had died. Another nearly did. And this was routine.

She leaned toward Ryan, who stood at her shoulder. "They're not going to do anything, are they?" she murmured.

Ryan exhaled slowly. "They'll file a report. Maybe. But Yenni's father has deep roots. Political favors. Family in the municipal government. His name won't land on a single page unless someone demands it from above."

Taylor glanced at the phone in her hand. On it—lots of footage. Audio recordings. Videos they'd taken after the incident. All of it organized, timestamped, and ready.

"Well," she said, sliding the drive into a padded envelope. "If they won't escalate it here, I will."

Ryan nodded. "Media?"

She nodded. "CNN. ABC. NYT. Even the travel bloggers.

Americans think these resorts are safe. They don't know how thin the walls really are."

Across the room, Aunt Heidi rushed in and clung to Madison like a woman saving someone from drowning—clutching her arms, stroking her hair, even though Madison seemed more focused on making sure the police officer could sense her disgust with him.

Taylor couldn't blame her.

Brady was pacing outside the glass doors, phone to his ear, probably calling the airline again, trying to get an earlier flight out. His jaw was tight, eyes flicking constantly toward the hallway like he expected someone else to come for them.

Ellis sat beside Cate in one of the corner armchairs. He looked ... aged. Ten years older than he had at the rehearsal dinner what seemed ages ago. His hands trembled slightly when he reached for his water bottle. Cate was rubbing his back gently, saying nothing.

He looked over and caught Taylor's eye. His expression softened.

"You were remarkable," he said hoarsely. "You both were."

Taylor followed his gaze to Sam, who stood at the table, arms crossed, flanked protectively near Gia. He hadn't left her side since they returned.

Something tightened in Taylor's chest. She'd always known Sam was strong, but what he showed over the past forty-eight hours wasn't just bravery. It was resolve.

She reached for his hand when he passed by her chair. He paused, glanced down at her, and gave it a squeeze. A silent connection passed between them.

She returned to her notes.

Her eye caught the small flash of movement near the door.

Rafael.

He entered quietly, hat in hand, head low. His uniform

looked too stiff, too pressed, like he was wearing it for a role he no longer believed in.

When he made it to her side, he didn't speak at first. Then—

"I'm sorry," he whispered. "I didn't know."

Taylor stood. Her voice was calm, but razor thin. "You didn't want to know. You didn't check your staff thoroughly. You let someone operate under the name Daniel when you have no Daniel on payroll. That wasn't oversight. That was willful ignorance."

Rafael looked gutted. "I can't connect the resort to this publicly. You understand that. I can make that an appeasing offer."

"I don't understand," she said. "I really don't."

He left a card on the table and walked out.

Sam came to stand beside her, nodding toward it. "That your invitation to never speak of this again?"

"Probably," she said, dropping it in the trash.

The local police finally stood and declared the interviews done. One of them handed Gia a blank sheet of paper and asked her to draw a map of the ranch. Gia blinked at it like it was a joke, then balled it up and threw it at him.

"We're done here," Taylor said, stepping between them and the girls. "You have the coordinates. If you want more information on details, you can request it through the attorney we will be securing for Madison and Gia."

The officers exchanged glances, then shrugged and left without argument.

Chaos slowly gave way to exhaustion. People began filtering out of the room, voices low, shoes scuffing tile.

"I'll meet you in the room," Sam said. "I'll get the first shower and be ready to give you a much-needed massage when you're through."

"I'm coming in a few minutes," she said.

But she stayed. Watching. Thinking. Her mind already racing through what would come next. Statements. Media releases. Ensuring Madison and Gia had access to legal representation and trauma counselors.

Ensuring Yenni's name was not forgotten.

She sat back in her chair and looked around at what was left of the celebration that had brought them all here.

A fairytale wedding in paradise.

And yet, outside the walls of paradise—truth, blood, and survival.

Chapter Twenty-Seven

The rhythmic click-click of Ginger's nails on the sidewalk was oddly comforting as Lucy stepped out of the parking garage onto West 72nd Street. The garage attendant, a middle-aged man in a Yankees cap, barely glanced at her as he waved a luxury SUV through the exit. The comforting chaos of New York City folded around her—horns honking, cyclists weaving between cars, tourists consulting maps and snapping photos.

It felt like stepping into an old pair of shoes, slightly worn but familiar and cozy.

She'd parked the Jeep in the closest long-term lot she could find, tucked between a dry cleaner with a faded awning and a bodega with a handwritten sign reading *Cash Only, ATM Inside*. She double-checked the door lock before slinging her backpack over one shoulder and adjusting Ginger's leash.

The dog's ears perked at the new smells and sounds, her tail wagging tentatively.

The Dakota loomed ahead, its weathered stone facade rising above the street like a silent sentinel. Its ornate arched entryway had always fascinated Lucy—the elegance, the history, the invisible boundary between those who belonged inside and those who only stood on the sidewalk staring, wondering.

She found herself drawn to the same bench she'd once sat on years ago, the one with the perfect view of the front entrance. She could still picture Edward, the elderly doorman with the warm smile, who used to sneak her bits of gossip and once slipped her a twenty-dollar bill just because he thought she looked hungry. Edward was nowhere to be seen, and she felt a flutter in her pulse, hoping he was still around somewhere, and not gone forever.

But Oscar was there. She spotted him within minutes, holding the door open for a delivery driver balancing an armful of fresh flowers. His face was leaner, more serious, but she'd know him anywhere.

Her fingers tightened on Ginger's leash. So much had changed. And so much hadn't.

She wondered about Suki's dogs—Bentley and Bailey, the spoiled French bulldogs who had their own matching raincoats and monogrammed bowls. Were they still around? If so, who walked them now? It felt like a lifetime ago that Lucy had slipped into Suki's orbit, circling her expensive life like a street rat who'd accidentally stumbled into a penthouse. And then stolen from it.

The memory made her stomach twist. Lucy had snuck away from Suki while she was in the bathroom, her cash crammed into the bottom of her backpack. She'd heard Suki's voice, slow and apologetic, talking through the bathroom door. Lucy hadn't stuck around long enough to hear every word, but she knew who Suki was talking to.

Ian.

And that meant Lucy hadn't had a choice. If Ian knew

where she was, it was only a matter of time before he came for Johnny.

But Suki had hated Ian. Maybe she'd forgiven her.

Or had Suki's extended family been the ones following Lucy all along? Making her feel watched. Crazy.

The park behind her was alive with summer—runners pounding the paths, tourists spreading out picnic blankets, children chasing bubbles. It made her feel even more out of place, her nerves too taut to fully absorb the simple joy of a city in bloom.

She was so lost in thought she almost didn't hear the soft rustle and grunt behind her.

When she turned, her heart caught in her throat.

Armina.

The older woman was exactly as Lucy remembered—her hair matted beneath the black and gold Versace scarf she wore like a crown, a faded baby doll cradled protectively in her arms. She muttered softly, her singsong Italian lullaby floating on the breeze as she dug through a trash can with her free hand.

"Armina," Lucy whispered, her voice catching on the name.

The woman didn't react at first, too caught up in her search. Lucy approached slowly, Ginger's ears pinned back, her tail uncertain. "Armina. It's me—Lucy."

Armina squinted at her, her weathered face creasing further in confusion. "Luce?" she finally murmured, uncertain.

"It's me," Lucy said softly. "I'm back."

Armina's eyes filled with something—recognition, sadness, maybe even relief—but she didn't smile. Instead, her gaze flickered toward the ground. Lucy couldn't tell if she recognized her or not.

When Lucy asked, "Where's Margot?" Armina's expression crumpled, and she shook her head side to side, her lips pursed tight.

Lucy felt her knees weaken. "She's gone?" she whispered. Guilt and grief curled hot and sharp in her stomach. *I left her. I left her here.*

But then, Armina raised her hand and pointed—down the sidewalk, toward the nearest hospital sign.

"Margot?" Lucy's voice cracked. "She's hospitalized?"

Armina nodded, then turned away, her lullaby starting up again as she shuffled toward the next trash can. Lucy stood frozen, torn between chasing after her and rushing to the hospital doors.

Ginger tugged at the leash, and it jolted Lucy back into motion.

"C'mon," she said urgently. "Let's go see if she's in there or if Armina is pulling our leg."

Quickly, she followed the sign to the next one, and then the next, until she saw the tall building and nearly ran the rest of the way.

Inside the emergency room, the fluorescent lights hummed too loud, the antiseptic smell sharp enough to sting her nose. A tired-looking nurse glanced up from behind the desk, her expression already prepared to tell Lucy to wait.

"I'm here for my mom," Lucy blurted. "Margot ... Margot Davis."

The nurse's face softened as she clicked the keyboard, then stood and gestured. "Right this way." She led Lucy through the double doors, down a hall, and into a room that held two beds with two patients.

The moment Lucy saw Margot, tears threatened to spill. Her once vibrant protector was thin, her skin pale and papery, her hair tucked under a ratty scarf. Her eyes, however, still held the spark of recognition.

"Lucy?" Margot's voice was hoarse with disbelief. "Where the hell have you been?"

Lucy took her hand, unsure what to say. "Around."

Margot gave her a knowing smile that didn't reach her eyes. "You look good, kid."

"You don't," Lucy said quietly, blinking back tears.

Margot sighed, her shoulders slumping. "Diabetes. It's kicking my ass. Keeping up with the insulin—when I can get it—isn't easy. Then I get all messed up and they keep me here until I'm stable, then kick me out." Her voice cracked with frustration. "My meds get stolen half the time. Can't keep insulin cold in a tent or under an overpass."

The nurse returned, her face apologetic. "I'm so sorry, but we're going to have to discharge you in about an hour. I'm glad your daughter is here because we need the bed for sicker patients, now that you are stable."

Lucy's temper flared. "She's not stable. She's homeless and sick—how the hell do you think this is gonna end? Or do you even care?"

The nurse's face remained impassive. "We do what we can. But do you? You're her daughter. Why is she in this shape in the first place?"

Lucy stood there, torn between fury and helplessness as Margot weakly swung her legs over the side of the bed, resigned to whatever came next.

"It's okay, kid. I'll make it. Always do, somehow."

This is what I left her to.

She couldn't do it again.

"Margot, you're not going back to a tent," Lucy said, her voice shaking with determination. "Or an overpass. Get dressed."

Margot's tired eyes widened in surprise, but she didn't argue.

She looked relieved that someone else would take charge of

her life, even temporarily. She was obviously still a very sick woman.

Lucy didn't know exactly what she was going to do next, but one thing was certain—Margot wasn't going back to the street. And maybe, just maybe, neither was Lucy.

Chapter Twenty-Eight

The alley behind The Dakota was slick with yesterday's rain, a thin sheen of grime coating the cracked pavement. Lucy glanced down at Margot, who leaned heavily against her side, her breathing shallow. Each step seemed to take more effort than the last, her weight sagging against Lucy's shoulder. Ginger trotted beside them, her ears flicking nervously at every sound.

"This is a bad idea," Margot muttered, her voice thin as tissue paper.

"It's the only idea," Lucy whispered back.

The service entrance door was propped open with a dented trash can, the scent of bleach and something fried drifting out. It had been years, but Lucy still knew this door like the back of her hand. She stepped inside, her breath held tight in her chest, and nearly collided with a man carrying a crate of wine bottles.

"Hey, watch it," he grunted, but barely spared them a glance.

That's when she saw him.

Edward.

He was thinner, his hair completely white now, but the softness in his eyes hadn't changed. The moment he spotted her, his wrinkled face split into a look of shock, followed quickly by something gentler—concern, maybe even affection.

"Lucy," he breathed, his voice a low whisper. "Well, I'll be damned. I thought I'd never see you again."

Her throat tightened, but she forced a shaky smile. "Hey, Edward."

"What're you doing here?" His gaze flicked to Margot, who was barely standing upright. "And where the hell have you been? You just up and disappeared like a wisp of smoke. Mrs. Banfield wouldn't speak of you either."

Lucy hesitated. There was no easy way to answer that.

Her silence was enough for him. For as long as he'd been a doorman, he could easily sense when discretion was needed. Questions to be left unanswered. He gave her a long, appraising look, then slowly nodded. "I didn't see you today," he said quietly, his words heavy with meaning.

Relief washed through her. "Thank you." She shifted Margot's weight, glancing toward the elevator. "Does Suki still live here?"

Edward's expression tightened, but he nodded. "I'm sure you've heard that Mr. Banfield passed away tragically. But Mrs. Banfield is still in the penthouse." His voice dropped even lower. "But you didn't hear that from me."

Lucy gave him a grateful smile. "You're a saint."

"Nah, just an old man with a soft spot for pretty girls," he muttered, watching as they shuffled toward the elevator. "Be careful, Lucy."

It wasn't about looks and she knew it. He wouldn't speak of it, but he'd never forget that she'd saved his job long ago, and, on top of that, gave him back his dignity when his boss was discriminating against him for being old.

Some people had no heart.

Every Little Thing

With the leash to Ginger in one hand, with the other she guided Margot in, and the ride up felt endless, the service elevator creaking with every floor. Lucy's heart pounded harder the closer they got to the top. By the time they reached the penthouse level, she was almost ready to turn around. Would Suki try to have her arrested? But then she looked at Margot—fragile, pale, eyes half-lidded with exhaustion—and squared her shoulders.

She knocked.

The door swung open to reveal Carmen, still trim and severe in her pressed uniform, her thick hair pulled into a tight bun. Her dark eyes widened, her mouth opening slightly in shock before she masked it with a tight scowl.

"Do I even want to know where you disappeared to?" Carmen asked, arms crossed. "Or should we go straight to what are you doing here—and who is that?" She nodded toward Margot.

Lucy swallowed hard. Lying wasn't as easy as it used to be. "It's my mother."

Carmen's eyes flicked from Lucy to Margot, her brow furrowing in clear doubt. "Your mother," she repeated, skeptical. But, after a long moment, she stepped aside. "Suki's not here, but she'll be back any minute. I'm telling her you bulldozed your way in. You deal with her. And leave that mutt outside."

Lucy nodded, nudging Margot forward into the familiar opulence of Suki's world. She let Ginger enter, too, ignoring Carmen's orders. Inside, a rush of moments hit her at once. Every detail was just as she remembered—the polished marble floors, the scent of expensive candles perfuming the air, the faint hum of the central air system that made the whole space feel like a cocoon. But before Lucy could get her bearings, a soft click-click-click sounded, and Bentley came trotting out, his tiny nails tapping the floor.

Ginger's hair stood up, but she let the dog sniff her and, when she realized he was harmless, she relaxed.

Bentley was wearing a Prada shirt, naturally, and the sight of him and all the extra gray around his muzzle made Lucy's heart squeeze painfully. "Hey, little man," she whispered, crouching down as he sniffed her hand, tail wagging. "Still the king of the castle, huh?"

His mate was nowhere in sight.

"Where's Bailey?" Lucy asked quietly, looking for Bentley's mate.

Carmen's expression flickered. "She passed last year."

Lucy swallowed the lump in her throat, her fingers curling in Bentley's soft fur. "I'm sorry you lost your sweetheart."

Carmen's tone softened just a touch and she led the way down the hall. "Come on, let's get your—mother—settled. And if that dog pees on my floors, you're cleaning them."

The tiny back room was exactly as Lucy remembered, with its narrow bed, modest dresser, and soft light from the window that overlooked Central Park. To Margot, it would feel like a palace.

Margot's eyes filled with tears as she collapsed onto the bed, exhausted beyond words.

Lucy turned to the housekeeper. "Carmen? Can you bring a nightgown?"

Carmen muttered something under her breath in Spanish, but she disappeared down the hall. Lucy knelt beside the bed, gently pulling Margot's shoes off, wincing at the sight of her cracked, filthy feet. One of her toes sported an angry blister.

"Oh, Margot, I'm so sorry," she whispered.

Carmen returned, arms full—nightgown, towels, a brush. Her mouth was set in a firm line, but something softened in her expression when she saw Margot's swollen feet. Without a word, she knelt and took her hand. "Come, Mamita. Let's get you cleaned up. A girl always feels better after a bath and some fresh clothes."

Margot's face crumpled in both embarrassment and gratitude, and a tear slid down her cheek before she looked away. Carmen's voice softened as she murmured gentle reassurances, guiding Margot to the bathroom like she was guiding a child.

Lucy stood alone for a moment, listening to the water running, Carmen's voice rising and falling in melodic Spanish. At least Margot could get cleaned up, maybe rest for a while.

This wasn't a long-term solution, but it was a start.

She wandered into the kitchen, trailing her fingers along the marble island, memories crowding in. She'd once sat here every morning, a cup of coffee beside her, her laptop and the latest gallery reports in front of her. Ian sitting across from her, sharp-eyed and always two steps ahead, teaching her how to read the market, how to anticipate the tastes of New York's elite. All the while demanding her to schedule this, fix that, and do everything to make his life easier.

He'd been cruel. Manipulative. But he'd also shaped her into something she never thought she could be—Lucia Leighton, the young and beautiful art consultant everyone trusted. Even now, her bank account bore the fruits of his training and what she'd used to become, back in her hometown.

Slowly, she moved into the living room and settled on the couch. Ginger curled up at her feet, waiting patiently for the next move.

Lucy felt so different just being in the penthouse.

She'd been someone special here, but it wasn't herself. She thought of Jorge, her Uruguayan artist with his soulful eyes and tender heart. He had believed in her when she didn't believe in herself. But he didn't know the real Lucy. He'd never guess that she'd slept on the streets, traded her body for food and drugs. That she'd become a rich man's mistress. Had his child, then nearly sold it to Ian. Her life was a long series of screw-ups and shame.

And she'd left him too. Like she left everyone.

She'd caught glimpses of his success in the years since—exhibitions, auction headlines, record-breaking sales. He didn't need her anymore. He probably hated her. Most likely he was married to a gorgeous model. Maybe a movie star.

Bentley jumped up beside her on the couch, curling into her lap, his warm body a surprising comfort. She rubbed his velvety ears, letting the soft texture soothe the storm inside her.

The sound of the front door opening made her sit bolt upright.

"Carmen," Suki's voice called out, sharp as ever. "Put Bentley's harness on. I want to—"

The footsteps stopped and that familiar slow and stoic voice rang out.

"Well, lookie here at what the cat dragged in."

Lucy slowly turned to face her, heart pounding in her chest. Suki stood in the entryway, sunglasses pushed up into her sleek dark hair, her expression unreadable.

The showdown had begun.

Chapter Twenty-Nine

Suki stared at Lucy for a long, quiet moment—eyes narrowed, lips pressed into a sleek, unreadable line. She crossed the room with calculated ease, tossed her designer bag on the entryway table, and unbuttoned her cream sweater like she owned every molecule of air in the penthouse.

"Carmen should've called security," she muttered without looking at her, tossing the sweater too.

Lucy stood her ground, arms crossed tightly. "Well, she didn't."

Suki let out a humorless laugh. "No, she didn't. She always did have a soft spot for you." She finally turned, her gaze sharp. "And I'll delay calling them myself. Because, despite everything, I'm still a sucker for a good story. And I want to hear yours."

Lucy exhaled, tension tightening the space between her shoulder blades. "You really want to talk about stories, Suki? Because last time we saw each other, you were playing one hell of a role. Talking to Ian through the bathroom door, planning to hand me and my baby over like some broken-down pet."

Suki's eyebrows arched, but she didn't flinch. "You heard that?"

Lucy nodded once. "Clear as glass. So don't act surprised that I walked out."

Suki paced to the wet bar, her long black hair swinging with the rhythm until she stopped and poured herself something clear—and probably expensive—and sipped. Her gold bracelets jingled softly as she leaned against the counter. "That's rich, coming from you. You walked out and dumped me in a hotel suite like I was the villain. You took my cash, my jewelry—"

"You were going to betray me," Lucy snapped, her voice tight. "You said you were on my side. But I was two feet from the door and already being sold out."

Suki's jaw clenched. For a moment, neither spoke.

Then, with a sudden bark of laughter, Suki raised her glass in Lucy's direction. "God, I forgot how sharp you are. That gut of yours—always on fire. I almost admire it."

"Almost," Lucy echoed flatly.

Suki tilted her head. "You do have nine lives, I' have to say. You reinvented yourself. Back in your charming backwoods hometown, right? Art director. Gallery coordinator. Whatever," she waved her arm in the air. "Peddling paintings for that eccentric medium woman, what's her name ... Faire?"

Lucy's lips parted, eyes narrowing. "How do you know that?"

"Oh, Lucy," Suki said sweetly. "You called me once, remember? From your own cell phone. You didn't block your number. Took me all of ten minutes to figure out where you'd landed. Not that I've looked you up recently. It's been ... what, a year?"

"You never came to Hart's Ridge?" Lucy asked slowly. "You never sent anyone? Never bugged the place?"

Suki rolled her eyes and set her drink down with a clink. "What do you think I am? KGB? Please. I've got much bigger fish to fry than chasing a former assistant turned hillbilly art whisperer."

Lucy's voice dropped, hoarse and low. "You swear to me ... you didn't send anyone?"

Suki leaned forward, the glint in her eyes edged with something jagged. "If I wanted you found, Lucy, trust me—you'd have been found. I'm many things, but I'm not your shadow."

Relief washed through Lucy in a sudden, choking wave—equal parts comfort and confusion.

But it didn't last.

Her voice dropped further, barely a whisper. "What about your parents?"

Suki blinked.

"They wanted Johnny," Lucy said. "He was supposed to be the heir, right? Ian's legacy. Are they following me? Watching my son?"

Suki didn't answer right away. She walked slowly to the balcony doors, her silhouette reflected faintly in the glass as she stared out at the city below.

"I don't know what they're doing," she said finally. "I cut them off after Ian died. They wanted me to return to Ukraine, take over the family's international assets, sit at the table with the old men and pretend I didn't know what they really were."

Lucy's stomach twisted.

Suki turned back to her, face carefully blank. "I'm making my own way now. And more money for myself than Ian ever made for them. So, whatever they're doing ... I don't want to know."

"So, it's possible," Lucy whispered. "That they're still watching. Still waiting."

"It's possible," Suki said, her tone dry. "It's also possible they've moved on to another heir. Or another scheme."

Lucy took a step back, her mind spinning. "That doesn't exactly help me sleep at night."

Suki shrugged. "I'm not here to help you sleep."

Silence stretched between them.

"I don't know what you think I am, Lucy. But, if you're looking for reassurances, you came to the *wrong* penthouse."

Lucy swallowed hard, her voice steadier than she felt. "I'm just trying to protect my son."

A flicker of something crossed Suki's face—regret? Pain?

"I'm glad you took him. I would've been a terrible mother," she said. "You know that, right? I've never seen what a healthy parent-child relationship even looks like. I grew up in a home where silence was a virtue and fear was currency."

Lucy stared at her, something old and soft flickering in her chest. Suki was damaged. Most of it inflicted by her own father and brother. Memories of growing up listening to her own father's drunken rages flew through her. Of Taylor trying to step in when Lucy cried herself to sleep, wanting her mother.

After a moment, she said quietly, "That's why I have to keep him safe. Because I know what it's like to grow up in fear. Different situations, but also hard."

Suki nodded once, almost imperceptibly.

"There's something else," Lucy said. "We both know how hard it is to be on our own, but we're lucky enough to have family resources if we choose to use them. I have a friend in dire need who isn't so lucky. Her name is Margot and she's ... sleeping. In the maid's room."

Suki blinked. "Margot? Who the hell is that?"

"A friend. From the streets. Years ago. She kept me alive when I first came to this city." Lucy swallowed hard. "She's real sick. Diabetic. She's been bouncing between hospitals and overpasses. I found her again. She has nowhere else to go."

Suki didn't answer. Her silence stretched again.

"I know what you're going to say," Lucy added, bracing herself. "I know you want us out. We can't stay here."

Suki tilted her head slightly, eyeing her like a curious cat.

"I'll leave, but I'm asking you to let her stay. Just until she gets her strength back."

"I might be a bitch," Suki said finally, rising from the chair. "But I'm not a cruel bitch."

Lucy blinked. "So ... she can stay?"

"For now." Suki smirked. "But I assume you're going to cover her rent. Especially since you still owe me for that little disappearing act and the bundle of money that vanished with you."

Lucy stiffened, color rising in her cheeks. "I don't have access to—"

"Spare me," Suki cut in, waving a manicured hand. "I'm not asking for cash. Not yet. But I do have a project. One you'd be perfect for."

Lucy's heart dropped.

Suki's smile widened—sharp and knowing.

"You're not going to like it," she added lightly, draining the rest of her drink. "But, then again, you never did shy away from danger, did you?"

Chapter Thirty

Suki poured herself another drink as if she had all the time in the world, the quiet chime of ice against crystal the only sound in the room.

Lucy stood stiff near the windows, her arms folded, heart thudding with unease. Bentley curled lazily on the couch, completely unfazed. Carmen had left for the day and Margot slept down the hall, but Lucy couldn't settle her nerves—not with whatever Suki was about to drop.

"I've got a job for you," Suki said at last, turning and sipping from her glass. "It'll clear your debt—the money you stole from me. It'll also cover your little friend's extended stay for some recovery time. And ... if you pull it off, you might just walk out of here with more than you bargained for."

Lucy's stomach tightened. "You already said that. I want to know what it is."

Suki smiled thinly. "We're going to stage a theft."

Lucy blinked. "A what?"

"A theft," Suki repeated, as if she were explaining a brunch reservation. "A very specific one. A painting. One Ian once owned, and one I want back. Quietly. Dramatically. And without the legalities of, you know—ownership."

Lucy stared. "You want me to steal a painting?"

"Not steal," Suki corrected. "Stage a theft. It won't go into circulation. It'll disappear for a while, let the buzz build, let the value increase. Then maybe it's recovered. Or maybe it's ... auctioned privately. Either way, I win."

"And me?"

"You get a fresh start. And the chance to protect that precious life you've rebuilt." Suki's gaze sharpened. "If my family really wants to, they can ruin your life. You think they won't find you forever, Lucy? You think you can hide your son under some dusty farm and dog rescue venture?"

Lucy flinched. She had been living a clean life. No drugs, drinking or crime. She really didn't want to turn back, but what choice did she have? She'd walked into a trap when she should've stayed away from Suki Banfield.

"Who owns the painting?"

Suki gave a slow, predatory smile. "Jackie Schafer."

For a moment, Lucy forgot how to breathe. "You're kidding."

"Do I look like I'm kidding?" Suki walked across the room and opened a drawer, pulling out a printed photo. She handed it to Lucy—a stark image of the painting in question: *Doll in Velvet* by Elio Verdan. The cracked porcelain face, the black velvet void. Lucy remembered it from where it hung in Ian's studio. She'd always hated the thing. Now, it made her skin crawl.

"She bought it at the Tokyo auction. The last event Ian ever showed at, God rest his soul," Suki winked, then went on. "She paid a fortune. And, trust me, she'll triple it in a few years. I've heard that she's locking it up soon. Once it goes into vault storage, it's untouchable."

Lucy was barely listening. Her mind spun with the name Jackie Schafer—Ian's old nemesis. Blonde. Ice-cold. All nails and cashmere and silent judgment. Lucy had met her only a handful of times during her days as Ian's assistant, but the woman had always made her feel like lint on a velvet coat.

"And how the hell am I supposed to get close to Jackie Schafer?" Lucy asked.

Suki's expression said *you already know*.

"No," Lucy whispered, already backing away. "No. I'm not going back there."

"You don't have to like it," Suki said. "You just have to be her. Lucia Leighton. Clean lines, curated knowledge, that particular blend of self-deprecation and ruthlessness. The art world misses you, darling."

Lucy shook her head. "She's not me anymore."

"She is you. Just a version you don't want to look at right now. Lucia is the version that can get close enough to Jackie. Become her best friend."

The silence hung thick between them.

Then Suki added, softly, "Besides ... Lucia is the only one who can walk into Jackie's world without raising questions."

Lucy's mouth was dry. "She won't trust me. I disappeared from the circuit."

"She doesn't have to trust you. She just has to invite you in. Want to make something off your success, like she always does."

Lucy rubbed a hand down her face, pacing to the far window. New York pulsed outside like a living thing. "And what happens if I get caught? What if someone recognizes me—really recognizes me?"

"Then you tell them the truth. You retreated from the NYC scene to have your child. Peace out, they call it. Tell them you took a new name—Lucy Gray—to stay under the radar and build your own portfolio. Get your own clients and not stay working with Ian. Or me. But now you're back. With some success under your belt." Suki set her glass down and folded her arms. "Jackie will eat it up."

Lucy turned back to her. "And what about Jorge?"

Suki raised an eyebrow. "What about Jorge?"

"If I re-enter that world ... he'll see me."

"Well," Suki said, not unkindly, "If he does, I suppose you'll find out if he's forgiven you for breaking his heart into a million pieces."

Lucy stood there, the weight of everything pressing against her chest.

Suki stepped closer. "Don't forget my family's unsavory, should we say, connections. Do you want to stay on the run forever? You want to raise your son with that fear etched into your skin?"

Lucy looked down at the photo of the painting again. The porcelain doll's eyes were blank, but she felt seen just the same.

"I'll need time," she whispered.

"You have four days," Suki said. "Jackie's hosting a private preview for select guests at a new exhibit she's sponsoring. I'll pull a few strings. And, voila! You're on the list."

Lucy nodded once, slowly. She got up and looked in the mirror, judging what she saw. She dreaded it, but Lucia Leighton was going to have to come out of retirement.

Chapter Thirty-One

The past few days had blurred into a strange rhythm of contradiction. Lucy's mornings began with walking Ginger and Bentley, then helping with Margot—checking her blood sugar, coaxing her to eat more than half a banana, making sure Carmen remembered to keep the insulin in the mini-fridge, not the main one. The maid's room was small but warm, and Carmen, despite her endless grumbling, had started bringing Margot tea and fresh pastries without being asked.

Once, Lucy even caught her singing under her breath as she helped Margot comb the tangles from her brittle hair.

Margot loved when Lucy came to sit with her and patiently listen to her stories. She wasn't used to television and had no use for it. Instead, she liked to talk, and she had so many tales of those she'd met in the park. Paths she'd crossed and people she still worried for. Sometimes Margot would slip into the deep past, and everything she'd gone through as a child, then a young adult, the trauma inflicted on her by her own family. Lucy listened, commented when necessary, and comforted however she could.

Margot was easy to be gentle with.

But as soon as Lucy closed Margot's door behind her, the softness vanished.

That's when she entered Suki's world. Lucia's world now too.

Ian's old office became a war room—whiteboards filled with names and galleries, exhibition schedules, and the latest social circles mapped like a military strategy. Suki walked her through the modern Manhattan art arena like a general preparing her best soldier for battle.

An event was coming up, and Lucia would make her reemergence there.

"You're not just walking into a party," Suki said, lounging on the velvet chaise with a flute of champagne. "You're stepping back onto a chessboard. And this time, you damn well better know who the queens are."

Lucia Leighton had to be reborn—not just in look, but in presence. Confidence. Curated style. The ability to deflect probing questions with elegance, and to whisper lies so softly they sounded like secrets.

Which was why, on a cold Wednesday morning, Lucy stood in front of Suki's full-length mirror wearing a dress she hadn't bought, in a life she wasn't sure she wanted back.

The sleek espresso bob Carmen had cut days earlier framed her face like a mask. Her makeup was perfectly balanced: not too dramatic, not too subtle. Just enough to say: *I've been through fire, and I came out lacquered in gold.*

Lucia's signature had always been cool control on the inside and Martha's Vineyard elegance on the outside. No bright colors. No oversharing. Calm and slow, her chin held high.

And absolutely no affection that couldn't be leveraged later.

Carmen stood behind her, arms crossed, frowning slightly.

"I guess Lucia is back," Lucy said, trying to joke, but it came out tight.

"I knew she'd be back," Carmen replied. "That's the problem."

In the past few years, Carmen had become a very close confidant to Suki. She knew more than she ever had now, and Suki made sure that her undocumented family was safe and well provided for—her reward for total allegiance.

However, Carmen was fond of Lucy too. Always had been.

She handed Lucy a light jacket—structured linen with gold buttons—and a leather handbag with the tags still inside. She whispered. "Be careful with Suki. She's not someone to trust, you know."

Lucy nodded once. "Neither am I."

She left the penthouse and hit the street like she belonged to it. Soon she was on Fifth Avenue, in awe as it shimmered with early afternoon summer light. Designer windows glittered with pre-spring florals lingering under the sharper scent of cold steel and sidewalk steam. Lucy strolled past Bergdorf Goodman, nodding at the window display of surrealist clutches, and ducked into Saks for a silk scarf she didn't need. She hoped it would work with a few outfits. Everything she bought needed to scream subtle wealth and curated power.

After a few hours of shopping, carrying bags of the latest summer suits and dresses, she stopped for lunch at a quiet café with panoramic windows that faced the Cartier Building—a place she remembered from her Ian days. The table was marble, the waitstaff efficient, and the silverware heavy with expectation.

She ordered a Niçoise salad and a sparkling water, then slid on her sunglasses and began scrolling through Artnet headlines on her phone. She needed to know what deals were happening, who was trending, and which artist was currently falling from grace.

She was halfway through an op-ed about a controversial installation in Prague when a cool voice cut through her thoughts.

"Well, well. If it isn't the ghost of Lucia Leighton. Here you were just added to the guest list for my private event tomorrow night and I see you today. What a coincidence!"

Lucy looked up, heart skipping—and then falling into rhythm again as she smiled. She wasn't quite ready yet, but here was her opportunity to open the door. Given to her on a silver platter.

Jackie Schafer stood there in dove-gray linen and diamonds so understated they somehow made the air cooler. Her blonde hair was swept into a twist so tight it could have been held together with willpower alone.

"Jackie, hello," Lucy said, smoothly falling into Lucia mode. "You look ... well rested."

Jackie gave a nonsmile and slid into the booth across from her. "Lucia, I thought you'd gone off-grid. Or joined a cult."

Lucy chuckled, her voice low and velvety. Unflustered. She could do this. All she had to do was channel the old Lucia. "A sabbatical. I needed perspective. The art scene here can be... devouring."

She titled her head, finger to her mouth. "Hmm ... don't I know it. But I heard you'd crashed. Spectacularly, actually."

Lucy let the pause hang just long enough then gave a chuckle. "Gossip doesn't look good on you, Jackie. But just to confirm, there was no crash. More like a recalibration. I did some work down south. Revived an overlooked artist's career. Curated a few intimate shows. Three sellouts, actually. Got me a few more artists to represent."

Artists that probably wonder how she'd dropped off the face of the earth by now.

Jackie raised a perfectly arched brow. "Really."

"I realized I'd spent too long under someone else's nameplate. I had to go off on my own, and now I only build things I own."

Jackie tilted her head. "Without Ian holding your leash."

Lucy's smile didn't waver. "Exactly."

"I told him he was wasting you," Jackie murmured. "But he always did hate being challenged."

Lucy took a sip of water. "His ego couldn't stand competition."

"Such a shame what happened to him, isn't it?" she asked, but didn't look that sorrowful. "A home invasion. How absolutely terrifying. They haven't found who did it yet either. I put a new alarm system in after that."

Noted, Lucy thought.

"And his poor wife," she continued, pretending to be empathetic.

She's his sister, but, guess what, Suki wasn't grieving either.

Jackie leaned in. "If you're really back, Lucia, then you're going to need visibility. Come to my preview. I'm showcasing pieces from my private collection. Very tight guest list."

"I'd love to," Lucy said, marveling internally about her luck.

Jackie's expression sharpened just a bit. "You remember *Doll in Velvet*?"

"Of course. How would anyone forget that piece? Ian used to have it, as I recall."

"That's right. It was his loss and it's not just a piece," Jackie said. "It's the centerpiece of everything I've seen in years. I plan to vault it soon, so this might be its last public appearance. It'll stay in hiding until it gains even more in value."

Lucy's pulse ramped up, but she didn't flinch. "A brilliant choice. People will talk."

"They always do. And what would they say if you and I started showing up together? You know, I could use an assistant, like you did for Ian."

She pretended to look offended then smiled slyly. "I'm beyond assistant work, Jackie. However, we might just make for a valuable twosome. Even help each other out. I know a few things now." She winked conspiratorially, then took a piece of paper from her purse and jotted her phone number on it. "I suppose I'll see you tomorrow evening."

Jackie stood gracefully and touched her arm before leaving. "That will be fun. I can't wait to see what you wear on that gorgeous body of yours. Any hints?"

"Thank you, but I haven't decided yet. Call it a surprise."

"Sounds intriguing. Well, it's been grand seeing you, Lucia. And I just have to say, it looks like this time ... you're playing to win."

Lucy didn't speak. Just nodded once.

She stayed at the table long after Jackie disappeared into the flow of Fifth Avenue, leaving behind the strong scent of Chanel.

Winning, she thought. Maybe so.

But then, this wasn't about winning.

This was about surviving.

———

Lucia Leighton may have taken control in the daylight, but, at night, Lucy Gray lay wide awake in Ian's bed. The mattress was too firm, the linens too pristine. Every creak of the walls felt like a breath held too long. The room hadn't changed much—same dark wood floors, same cold gray walls, same masculine furniture that screamed control and ego. Even the scent of his cologne still lingered faintly in the closet, like a ghost that refused to move on.

She hated being in there. But the guest room was being used to store Suki's gallery acquisitions, and Margot had the maid's quarters. So Lucy had been given his room. His bed.

It didn't help that Suki insisted on calling it "the principal suite," like Ian had never existed at all. With Lucy's luck, he was still there, watching every move she made, waiting for the moment to haunt the hell out of her.

Ginger shifted at the foot of the bed, then let out a low, unsettled whine.

"Shhh," Lucy whispered, rolling over. "It's fine."

Ginger whined again. Then again—louder this time. She got up, circled twice, and started nudging the covers around Lucy.

Lucy groaned, rubbing her eyes. "Girl, what is it? You went out at midnight. No way you need to go again."

But Ginger didn't stop. This time she nipped at Lucy's toes through the sheet, something she'd never done before. Something was wrong.

"Ow! Okay, okay, I'm up."

Lucy sat up, squinting in the dim light spilling in through the cracked door. She slipped out of bed, the wood floor cool under her feet. Her first thought: *An intruder?*

She padded down the hallway in her silk robe, heart ticking faster with each step. She peeked into the main living area. Nothing. The security system was armed—green light steady. Bentley was curled in his plush designer bed by the fireplace, snoring softly. Not a threat in sight.

Lucy moved toward Suki's room and gently turned the handle. Locked.

Typical.

When she heard nothing from the other side of the door, she turned toward the small hallway that led to the maid's room.

"Margot?" she called softly, not wanting to wake her if she was sleeping.

No answer. Ginger whined louder this time.

Lucy cracked the door and peeked inside.

Margot lay tangled in her sheets, her skin slick with sweat, her breathing shallow. Her eyes were half open, unfocused, and her hands twitched like she was trying to grasp at air.

"Oh my God," Lucy breathed, heart slamming into her ribs as she rushed in.

"Margot!" She went to her side and shook her gently. "Hey, come on, open your eyes. Look at me."

Margot moaned, barely coherent, her mouth moving but no words coming out.

Lucy felt her forehead—clammy. Cold. The half-eaten orange and a plate of carrots from earlier sat on the nightstand, mostly untouched. Margot had to eat before going to sleep for the night. They'd found that out the hard way.

A repeat was before her. This time Margot looked sicker.

"Shit. You're crashing." She bolted from the room and sprinted to the kitchen, flinging open drawers and cabinets until she found the emergency glucose gel and Margot's backup meds.

Carmen had stuck them on a high shelf, far from reach.

"Dammit," Lucy hissed, stretching for them and grabbing a juice box and a cookie on her way back to the room.

She propped Margot up as best she could, speaking in calm, clipped tones.

"Wake up, Margot! I need you to drink this, okay? Just a few sips."

She didn't respond.

Margot's lips were dry, but Lucy managed to coax the straw into her mouth. A little of the juice went in. Then a little more. Lucy slipped a cookie into her hand, broke off pieces, and helped her chew.

Her skin started to warm slightly. Her breathing evened.

Lucy sat beside her on the edge of the narrow bed, heart still hammering. She stroked Margot's hair, whispering, "You're okay. You're okay. I've got you."

After a few minutes, Margot's fingers twitched again—this time with a little more purpose. She opened her eyes.

"You're back," Lucy said, letting out a shaky laugh. "Scared the hell out of me."

Margot blinked, still groggy. "You came ... You came back."

"Yeah," Lucy murmured. "I'm not going anywhere. Not tonight."

But as she sat there, rocking ever so slightly, something heavy settled in her chest.

This wasn't sustainable.

Margot needed someone to check her levels several times a day. She needed a place where her insulin was always kept cold, where her food was consistent, where people didn't sleep so far away that they couldn't hear her in time.

Lucy had barely saved her tonight. What if Ginger hadn't woken her?

And what if Margot crashed while she was out playing pretend as Lucia Leighton?

She looked down at her friend—this woman who had taken her in once, protected her from the cold, from men, from monsters—and now it was Lucy's turn. But she would have to leave eventually. Back to Hart's Ridge. To her son.

She had to.

Which meant she needed to figure something more permanent for Margot. Fast. Before time ran out. Before their luck did.

She sat in the chair next to her until the sun began to rise, Ginger curled at her feet, Bentley now awake and peeking around the corner like he knew something serious had just passed.

Lucy didn't go back to Ian's bed.

She stayed right where she was.

Chapter Thirty-Two

It was mid-morning, Lucy had changed out of her robe and into a nice track suit, her hair still damp from the fastest shower of her life.

Margot was stable—for now. During the day, Carmen was hovering over her like a grumbling guardian angel, brewing tea and muttering in Spanish under her breath while keeping a close eye on her patient between her many other tasks.

At night, Lucy had ordered a cot to arrive next-day-express and slept by her side.

"She needs someone to live with her 24/7," Carmen finally said, not bothering to lower her voice. "And if you're leaving soon, that someone isn't going to be you."

Lucy nodded, guilt spreading like smoke through her ribs. "I know."

"Suki keeps me too busy. I cannot be her nurse either," Carmen added, her tone softening. "I'm barely getting my work done, and you know, if I miss something, Suki will be on me. I'm doing my best here, Lucy, but I'm tired."

"I'll figure out something."

After breakfast, she slipped into Ian's office—the war room—

and pulled out her laptop. She spent the next hour calling every halfway house, assisted living program, and women's shelter she could find. Most had waiting lists. Some required referrals. A few wanted money up front, more than Lucy could give without revealing her location.

She wrote names down anyway. Circled the ones that might work. Underlined a private clinic in New Jersey that took sliding-scale patients but only had one bed left.

Her mind spun in two directions—half on Margot, half on Jackie Schafer's art preview that evening.

She needed to be there. It wasn't just about the painting anymore. It was about proving she could still slip back into Lucia Leighton like nothing had happened. It was about freeing herself and Johnny from the connection to Ian's father. But Suki was going to have to sweeten the terms. If Lucy played this right, she might even find a way to fund Margot's care long-term.

One heist. One act of deception. And maybe she could save them both.

Taylor's face came to mind, complete with a disapproving expression. But Lucy couldn't afford to let her sister unintentionally guilt her and make her continue walking a straight line. Taylor couldn't possibly understand how high the stakes were.

She stood, looking at the time on her phone. It was time to start preparing for the evening. For this one, she needed to be well rested and perfect. Not rushed and weary. Too much depended on her making just the right return to the circles that would just assuredly rather chew and spit you out than welcome you with open arms.

———

The event was held at a private gallery in Chelsea—a converted warehouse with exposed brick, ambient lighting, and enough name tags to start a luxury army. Lucy arrived precisely at 7:14 p.m., fashionably late, dressed in a midnight-blue satin gown by Faviani that hugged her curves like it had been sewn there. It had set Suki back seven hundred dollars but was a bargain for something special enough for the event. Lucy's hair was pulled back in a soft twist, a pair of Suki's antique earrings glinting at her jaw.

Jackie Schafer met her at the door with a glass of champagne and a calculating smile.

"You showed," she said, offering the flute as she looked her up and down. "Love the dress."

"Of course I showed," Lucy replied, slipping into place beside her. "I wouldn't miss the resurrection of my New York reputation at such an elite gathering."

Jackie laughed lightly. "I hope it's not a resurrection. That would imply death. Remember, you were just ... hibernating."

Lucy sipped her drink, thinking of Ian's tragic demise that immediately followed her exodus, most likely at the hands of his sister. "Something like that."

They made the rounds together—shaking hands, exchanging ridiculous air kisses, discussing market value and international scarcity. Lucy played well for Jackie's favors. She also faked admiration for a monochrome sculpture, complimented a critic's new book she hadn't read, and managed to drop Ian's name only once.

Strategically, of course.

Everything was going smoothly—until she saw him.

Jorge Vanzo.

Her breath caught and her chest moved visibly with the rush of adrenalin through her body, her visceral response to a man who had made her want to believe in happily ever afters for a short time. A man who she'd dropped without explanation, as though he meant no more to her than changing her mailing address, though her soul knew better.

He stood near the far wall, in front of a minimalistic triptych of abstract reds and golds. His hair was longer than she remembered, pulled back at the nape of his neck. His suit was charcoal and fitted his lean body like a glove. He wore no tie, and his hands were tucked into his pockets like he was keeping them from reaching for something—or someone.

He turned.

Their eyes met. His deep and broody.

And just like that, the years collapsed between them.

She didn't move. Couldn't.

Jorge's expression shifted—recognition, disbelief, then something darker. He blinked slowly, like trying to erase her with his lashes. Then he turned and walked away.

Lucy swallowed hard and reached blindly for the champagne glass, suddenly wishing it were something stronger.

"You okay?" Jackie asked, noticing her face.

"Fine," Lucy said. "Just spotting a ghost."

"Funny," Jackie said, sipping from her own glass. "I was about to say the same. He's my star guest, as a matter of fact. Can't believe I got him here."

Lucy forced a smile, but her gaze tracked Jorge until he vanished into the crowd.

Later, while the guests buzzed around the wine bar and dessert trays, Jackie led a small group to the featured piece—*Doll in Velvet*.

It stood alone under a spotlight, its haunting cracked-doll face catching the light like porcelain skin.

Lucy stared at it too long, pulse fluttering in her neck.

"This is the one I told you about," Jackie announced to the group. "Privately acquired. Never been on public display."

Lucy leaned in, her tone reverent. "It's even more chilling in person."

Jackie turned to her with a gleam in her eye. "It's going to the vault next week. And not the kind you rent by the month, darling. The kind no one talks about."

Lucy smiled, looking exceptionally believable in her earnestness. "Good. Let it rest. Pieces like this ... they deserve silence."

But in her gut, she knew silence wouldn't last forever.

Jackie wouldn't own it for long, if she had anything to do with it.

Back at the penthouse that night, long after the heels came off and the dress had been hung back in its plastic, Lucy stood at the edge of Margot's bed.

The woman was asleep, her breathing slow but steady. A soft wheeze. Carmen had braided her hair and left a fan running nearby. On the nightstand sat a small bouquet of fresh lavender and a plate with toast crumbs. A tiny jar of sugar-free jam.

Lucy sat gently on the edge of the bed, fingers curled around her own thoughts. Thoughts about Jackie. And the painting. If she pulled this off—this job, this ridiculous scheme—Margot could be safe. She could be cared for.

And Lucy could go home to Johnny without the weight of uncertainty crushing her ribs.

But Jorge ... his eyes haunted her more than the porcelain doll ever could. They couldn't keep crossing paths because she hadn't known how much it would hurt to see him walk away.

She wasn't sure she'd survive it if he turned back around.

Chapter Thirty-Three

The door creaked open, and the sunlight poured in like a benediction. Taylor stepped outside with Sam and Lennon, blinking against the brightness of home. The warmth of the Georgia sun kissed her cheeks, and, for a breath, it was all she could do not to cry with relief.

It was cliché, but oh so true.

There was no place like home.

The back porch was strung with mismatched fairy lights and the familiar scent of hickory smoke, honeysuckle, and baked beans curled through the air. The screen door thumped gently shut behind her. Sam shifted Lennon to his other hip as the baby squealed and pointed to the flurry of activity just beyond the steps.

They'd only been inside a few minutes, but now—suddenly—everyone was here.

It was as if the whole town had arrived in their back yard while she'd caught her breath. But, no, this was family. Everyone she cared about. Except Lucy.

Taylor stood still, just watching.

Jo was in her element, overseeing the catering spread like a general, with Mabel at her side hollering instructions at Quig, who was shuffling a tray of buns dangerously close to the edge of the buffet table.

"Careful, Quig!" Jo snapped. "You drop those rolls, and I will make you eat 'em off the grass."

Quig just grinned, snuck a corn cob off one of the platters, and shoved it whole into her mouth before heading toward the ice chest like she hadn't just committed an act of carbohydrate theft.

Cecil saw her get away with it and grabbed his own cob, only to have it plucked from his hands by Mabel, who stood there glaring.

"Did I call y'all to eat yet? Don't think you'll be gumming that cob before we say the blessing, anyway."

Cecil lay his head back and laughed, all the way from the belly. A sound that Taylor missed right up there almost as much as the sound of Lennon's babbling. How she loved that man.

Adele—Taylor's sassy grandmother—was at the long folding table, setting out paper plates and napkins with meticulous care. Her floral apron flapped in the breeze, her steel-gray hair short and neat, as usual.

She glanced up and saw Taylor, and her entire face softened. Adele wasn't one for flowery words or mushy hugs.

She didn't speak, just gave a single nod like, *you made it home.*

Taylor nodded back.

On the far side of the lawn, Levi was whooping and swinging a fraying rope above his head, trying to lasso the fake calf they set out for the kids during barbecues. His jeans were half in and half out of his cowboy boots, his T-shirt dusty, and he was hollering like he'd just come off a rodeo circuit.

"Reckon he thinks he's in Texas," Sam murmured beside her, grinning.

From Texas to the Caribbean in one door slam, Johnny came running out with Alice behind him.

"He wanted to wear his pirate costume," Alice said, looking exasperated.

"It's fine," Sam said. "Let the pirate and the cowboy figure it out."

They laughed and Alice came and took Lennon, and began walking around with her on her hip, teasing her with kisses.

Near the old porch swing, Corbin sat cross-legged with his dog at his feet, a battered acoustic guitar in his arms, gently strumming chords that sounded like summer and memory all rolled into one. Sutton sat beside him on a quilt, leaning into his shoulder, eyes closed, a look of complete peace on her face.

It was a painting. A living, breathing canvas of everything Taylor had missed.

And then she saw them—Anna standing just off the path, her kids on either side, holding her hands like they were afraid she might float away again. Her expression was pinched, her eyes tired. Hazard wasn't with her, and she looked like she could feel the weight of his absence like a missing limb. Still, Anna's arms were full, her children clinging to her for once, their cheeks pressed to her waist, their faces lighting up every time she looked down. Despite their sometimes-bad manners, they'd missed their mama.

Just like Lennon and Alice had missed her and Sam.

Taylor felt her chest ache—not from sadness, but from the strange tenderness of survival.

Then came the unmistakable click-click-click of dog nails on the wooden planks.

Diesel.

He bounded out of the kitchen with a low chuff, tail wagging low and fast, his amber eyes searching until he locked on Taylor with laser focus. He skidded to a halt in front of her, sat, and pressed his nose to her thigh like he had to be sure she was real.

As he had every five minutes since she'd arrived home.

"Hey, buddy," she whispered, dropping a hand to his head, fingers tangling in his thick coat. "I'm not going anywhere for a while. Just relax."

Behind him, Ginger—Lucy's hound—trotted out, ears flopping, tongue lolling. She gave Diesel a quick sniff, then loped off toward the kids.

Diesel didn't move. He wouldn't. Not now and not until her safe return had worn off. Not after Taylor had disappeared into danger without him. Somehow, he'd sensed it.

He was her shadow again, and she welcomed it.

Then she spotted him.

Her father.

Jackson was standing near the grill, talking to Sam's dad who had come down for the reunion—but it was clear he wasn't really listening. His face was red, the kind of red that came from more than just the sun, and he held a cup that was definitely not sweet tea. His movements were fidgety, his laughter too loud, too sharp.

Taylor's stomach twisted.

Sam noticed too. "You think he's drinking again?"

"I know he is," she sighed. "He always does when things get too big for him to hold. He's really worried about Lucy. He called me this morning about her."

Always Lucy.

Her dad would never care about her the way he did his youngest daughter. Now that she had Sam, Alice, and Lennon, it didn't hurt as bad. But she still didn't want to see him going down that road again. She didn't have the energy to try to keep him alive as she'd done for so many years before. And Lucy sure as hell wasn't going to have any compassion for anyone but herself. If she had, she wouldn't have left Johnny like she had.

Sam adjusted Lennon, whose head was now nestled against his chest. "You want me to talk to him?"

Taylor shook her head. "No. Let him have today. Let him believe we're not watching. I'll talk to Cecil. See how he thinks we should handle it."

She tried to push it out of her mind and enjoy the day.

Across the yard, Gia stood with Madison and Brady, her arm linked with Madison's like they'd known each other their entire lives. Gia looked tired but grounded, like she'd started the first step of a thousand-mile walk and wasn't turning around. Brady had one hand on Madison's back and the other on a plate piled high with ribs—clearly doing his best to stay quiet and supportive and out of trouble.

Cate and Ellis were seated in the shade, their chairs close together. Ellis looked older than he had when they'd left for Mexico. His face was thinner, eyes sunken, his movements more deliberate. But he looked lighter too—like the burden had finally found a place to rest.

Taylor caught his eye and smiled. He smiled back.

For a long moment, she let it all wash over her. The clatter of dishes. The music. The dogs weaving between knees. The kids shrieking as Levi finally roped the fake calf and declared himself a rodeo king. The smell of honeysuckle and barbecue smoke and the almost holy hum of being home.

She turned to Sam and leaned into his side. "You think they all know how close we came to not coming back?"

He looked down at her, eyes warm. "Maybe not. But we do."

Taylor kissed Lennon's head and exhaled.

"Then let's make sure we never forget."

Chapter Thirty-Four

The sun was barely up, yet Central Park was already moving. Lucy walked slowly along the path with Bentley tugging toward every pigeon and scent patch, and Ginger beside her at a more dignified pace. It was a nearly perfect summer morning, the slight breeze kissing her skin and giving her a warm hug.

All around her, the park stirred to life like a stage production coming into focus. Across the lawn, a yoga class was forming—early risers in matching leggings unrolling their mats with meditative precision. Further down, a vendor was setting up his cart, the smell of hot pretzels and coffee wafting faintly through the air. A jogger passed her in silence, earbuds tucked in, his stride methodical.

But what caught Lucy's eye—what always caught her eye—were the others. The invisible ones.

Clusters of tents had been scattered behind a group of trees, barely visible unless you knew where to look. Ragged tarps, cardboard, the occasional sleeping bag. Human silhouettes shifted within them—some already packing up, others slow to wake.

Every Little Thing

She watched as two NYPD park officers approached from the main path, their pace relaxed but deliberate. One of them was holding a radio to his shoulder, murmuring something Lucy couldn't hear.

Wordlessly, like a silent dance, the scattering began.

A man folded up a tent with expert speed. A woman in a knit hat threw a blanket over her shoulders and stood, face tilted toward the sun as she stretched, then turned to roll her sleeping bag. Another man—stooped and grizzled—strapped on a guitar case like it was armor.

Lucy's throat tightened.

Mike.

She remembered him. His fingers were calloused and worn, but, when he played at night, the world grew quiet. She and Margot had listened, sitting cross-legged in the dark, sipping stale coffee someone had donated. Some of them with something stronger.

There had been laughter. Harmony.

Not perfect, but enough.

Enough for their circle of misfits to feel human again. Enough to show Lucy on those nights that the displaced people among her were just like everyone else. They had hopes and dreams, mostly shattered from the hard knocks of life, but they held onto faith. They held that tiny strand so tightly, navigating through days and nights of hunger and uncertainty, through ridicule and harassment, continuing a path that they hoped led to something better.

Why had she been born so lucky? And not these people?

It wasn't fair.

Bentley snorted at a squirrel and Ginger gave a little yip of protest. Lucy kept walking, tears stinging her eyes.

She passed a bench where Armina once held court—wrapped in her old black and gold Versace scarf, cradling her porcelain baby doll as if it were real, singing lullabies in Italian under her breath.

"*Dormi, dormi, bel bambino ...*"

Lucy could still hear the song sometimes in her dreams.

Armina had once been a midwife in Queens, or so was said. Lucy believed her. She spoke too confidently about birth, too gently to be a liar. Something had snapped when her family sent her away—called her "unstable," refused to help her after her diagnosis. Her eyes never quite focused, but there was peace in her delusion. She was kind. Safe. And still had her dignity, in her own way.

How could anyone throw that away?

Lucy's hands tightened around Ginger's leash as Bentley paused to sniff a discarded newspaper. Every step she took filled her with dread. Every shadowed corner of the park whispered *what if that's Margot next week?*

What if she ends up back here ... and doesn't wake up one night?

How was she supposed to go home, kiss her son's forehead, and sleep at night knowing Margot—who had once given her the last cup of hot coffee in a thermos and shelter when she had none—was curled beneath a bridge somewhere, her body giving out one tremor at a time?

Lucy's phone buzzed. A text message.

She fumbled in her pocket, expecting Suki, or Carmen.

Instead, the name lit up like a wound.

Jorge Vanzo.

Her thumb hovered.

Then she opened it.

> I saw you last night. I don't know what hurt more—seeing your face or remembering how much I loved you. Can we talk?

Lucy stared at the message; her breath caught in her throat. The dogs shifted beside her, pulling gently on their leashes.

Behind her, the police moved through the trees, now helping an older man stuff his belongings into a trash bag. Lucy recognized the look in his eyes—the same one Margot had when she was lucid enough to ask, "Where will I go next?"

She didn't answer Jorge.

She couldn't—not yet.

Instead, she lowered herself onto the nearest bench and let the dogs rest at her feet. She watched the yoga instructor lead the class through downward dog, watched the joggers loop the path with smooth repetition.

Then she looked out over the place where she had once slept. Where she'd hidden. Where she'd healed.

And now, the woman who had helped her survive it might not survive without her.

You're going to have to choose soon, she thought.

Chapter Thirty-Five

Margot was spinning a tale about a wedding. She lay on top of the covers, her limbs frail but animated, gesturing with one hand as Lucy sat beside her on the edge of the narrow bed. "He had a green tuxedo," Margot was saying, eyes wide with delight, "green like dollar bills, with a peacock feather in his pocket square. And the bride wore a dress made entirely of silk scarves. One from every country they'd ever slept in."

Lucy smiled softly, brushing a strand of hair back from Margot's cheek. "Sounds ... colorful."

"Oh, baby," Margot crooned, "you should've seen the cake. It was three tiers of tiramisu, and, I'm telling you, the top tier had a little carousel that spun really slow."

"Did it play music?" Lucy asked.

"Of course it did. Stevie Wonder. 'Isn't She Lovely.'"

Margot faded off then, the details slipping into a hum. Lucy stayed a few minutes longer, listening to the rustle of the city beyond the walls, the dogs snoring faintly in the other room. For all her wild stories, Margot's mind still shone when it sparked.

But Lucy could see the decline too—the deeper dips in clarity, the longer silences afterward.

Time was running out.

She stood, kissed Margot's forehead, and stepped out into the hallway. The door clicked shut behind her and Lucy tiptoed away.

Ian's office still smelled like him, and it held a heavy energy.

She crossed to the desk, pulled her Georgia phone from the bottom drawer, and hesitated. The screen was smudged, the battery barely holding a charge. She hadn't powered it on in weeks.

One tap.

It lit up like a flare. Thirty-six missed calls, several voicemails, and a handful of messages, many from Taylor and her sisters. A few from Cate.

And, of course, her dad.

While she scrolled through messages, she snooped through other drawers on the desk. In the file drawer, she found a folder with Ian's handwriting still on the tab. She opened it to find a list of art pieces that had gone on to Ukraine, along with the shipping address.

She wondered if they were stolen. She knew that Ian used paintings to launder money, but was he into theft too? If so, he had hidden that part from her. And if he was stealing art and sending it to Ukraine, then there was the trail. She'd have to look up the numbers and see.

Quickly, she pulled the papers from it, folded them until it was just a small square, and pushed them down into her blouse.

She went back to her own messages. A Leena Raines had called, left a message and texts. The last text was a photo. A painting, rough but arresting. Vibrant brushstrokes, the shape of a woman with her face blurred by a red sash. It screamed boldness. Rawness.

Lucy scrolled up to the voicemail from Leena—nervous, but hopeful.

"I know you're probably too busy, or maybe you're not doing this anymore, but ... I just wanted to show you what I've been working on. You believed in me before, and, if you ever want to rep someone new, I think I'm finally ready."

Lucy's pulse picked up. The work was good. Good enough, maybe, to bait someone like Jackie Schafer into letting her in again—this time, on her own turf.

She picked up the desk phone and dialed.

Jackie answered after two rings. "Lucia. So soon?"

"I wouldn't usually bother you the morning after your event," Lucy said, warmth coating her words, "but something came across my desk that I think you'll want to see. A new artist. Fierce, female, bold. The kind of risk you always say you're craving."

Jackie paused.

"I could swing by and show you her portfolio. I know you keep a busy schedule, but—"

"Come by this afternoon," Jackie said smoothly. "I'm in the mood to be impressed."

"Perfect," Lucy said, eyes narrowing. "I'll bring the kind of work you won't want going to someone else."

Lucy hung up and turned—only to find Suki leaning against the doorframe.

She hadn't heard her come in.

"How much of that did you hear?" Lucy asked warily.

"All of it." Suki's smile stretched across her face, delighted. "And I have to say ... that was impressive."

Lucy leaned back on the desk. "I'm not doing this for you, just so you know."

"Of course not," Suki said silkily. "You're doing it for her." She tipped her head toward the hallway. "Your little houseguest. But make no mistake, Lucia, you aren't any better than I am. Or Ian was. You know that you have a rebellious little streak that is egging you on, telling you this will be the ultimate thrill."

Lucy's jaw tightened. Maybe she did have that, but, if she did, she didn't like it.

"Well," Suki continued, walking slowly into the office. "If this works, and you can really get into Jackie's place again before she locks up that doll-faced monstrosity ... we might have to consider other partnerships. I have a list of clients who would kill to have your finesse."

Lucy forced a smile and lied. "I'll think about it."

But she wouldn't. Not for a second.

Even if Suki had cut ties with her monstrous family, even if she wasn't feeding Johnny's location to them in secret, Lucy couldn't take the risk. Not with her son's life on the line. Complete separation was what she needed.

She dressed fast—neutral heels, a tailored navy blouse tucked into beige trousers, a camel trench thrown over the top. Chic, classy, not too eager. She used Ian's printer and slid printouts from Leena's work into her leather portfolio, touched up her makeup, and kissed Ginger on the nose.

"You be good," she whispered. "I'll be back."

Bentley, predictably, ignored her. Too busy chasing something in his sleep. He grunted and farted, and Lucy laughed at Ginger's expression.

"Yes, my girl. That's a man for you."

She called an Uber and waited downstairs. The driver was a middle-aged man named Larry who wouldn't stop talking.

"Big meeting?" he asked. "You look like you're about to run the world."

"Something like that," Lucy murmured, eyes locked on the window.

"I had a woman once. Big shot in real estate. Used to take

meetings in sweatpants. Said it made men underestimate her. You ever do that?"

"I'm a fan of tailoring," Lucy said.

He laughed. "Hey, to each their own, right?"

She nodded absently, her mind already ten blocks ahead.

By the time they pulled up in front of Jackie's building—an understated high-rise with a discreet gold awning—Lucy was nearly vibrating with nerves. She tipped Larry too much just to get rid of him without waiting for his current story to end, then turned and walked inside.

The lobby was marble and silence. An elevator whisked her to the penthouse floor, and Jackie opened the door herself, a flute of something pale already in her hand.

"You're punctual," she said.

"As everyone should be," Lucy replied.

Jackie swept her in with a wave. "Come in. Let me give you a tour first. I just acquired a vintage Italian console I'm absurdly proud of."

The apartment was a modern palace—glass, brass, and stone. Sculptures posed on pedestals, paintings tastefully spotlighted, textiles too fine to sit on. Lucy let herself be led from room to room, nodding and complimenting, calculating every step.

"So," Lucy said carefully, "is *Doll in Velvet* still out?"

Jackie smiled, all teeth. "For another day or two. Then it goes to the vault. A room with all my most prized possessions. Not just art—though it's climate controlled. I call it the Golden Room, and only three people have the code, and I'm not one of them. Insurance won't let me."

Lucy didn't believe that for a minute. She arched a brow. "So, it's like Fort Knox?"

"Exactly. And once a piece goes in, it stays there until it hits the market again."

Lucy forced herself not to exhale. She had to move fast.

Jackie led her to the sunroom, where they sat and reviewed Leena's prints. Jackie was interested. Very interested.

"Hmm ... I think you might be on to something, Lucia," she mused. "But why do you want to share your find with me?"

"First, I've got my hands full with my current clients and also I don't have the riches clients like yours do."

Jackie smiled slyly. "Yes, I suppose you're right. I could host a salon showing," she mused. "Test her with a few buyers. If she passes muster, maybe she gets a seat at the table."

"That's what I thought," Lucy said smoothly. "I can help with that, and you barely have to lift a finger. I've gotten very good at hosting these events."

"Well, you said you were beyond assistant duties, so I wasn't going to ask, but if you are offering ..."

"I'd be happy to, Jackie." Her mind was already spinning. "And maybe you could let the painting be shown one more time. Really build the interest by saying 'last glance from the public eye' or something like that." The clock was ticking on the painting. On Margot. On her ability to hold this whole performance together without slipping.

"I like that," she replied, nodding emphatically. "That painting can be my retirement, once it ages a bit longer."

As Jackie poured them both another drink, Lucy smiled and leaned back, appearing perfectly at ease.

But, inside, she was already plotting the next move.

Chapter Thirty-Six

The day was warm, the kind of lazy spring heat that made the curtains drift like breath. Lennon had finally gone down for her afternoon nap, her cheeks pink from the soft Georgia sun streaming through the window. Taylor sat curled up on the worn couch in her leggings and a faded tee, half-reading a magazine she wasn't absorbing, her ears tuned to the monitor on the table beside her.

Outside, bees hummed around the porch roses, and Diesel lay sprawled like a bear rug in the kitchen doorway, his ears twitching at the smallest sound. It was peaceful. The kind of peace she'd begged for after Mexico. The kind of peace she wasn't sure she deserved.

Then came the knock.

It was firm but not urgent—three easy, measured taps. Familiar.

She froze for a moment, heart ticking into overdrive like she hadn't fully decompressed yet. Then she rose and crossed the floor, Diesel immediately on her heels, alert.

She opened the door to find Sheriff Dawkins standing on the porch, hat in hand, boots coated in fresh red dirt.

"Sheriff," she said, surprised. "Come on in."

"Afternoon, Taylor." He tipped his hat. "Didn't mean to drop in, but I figured, if I waited for the right time, I'd miss you entirely."

"Sam's at the lake with the kids. Just me and Lennon. She's napping."

"Then I'll make it quick," he said. But the way he stepped inside told her it wouldn't be.

Taylor offered coffee. He declined. He always did.

He settled into the corner chair, the one with the creaky leg and faded blue cushion. He used to sit in that same chair when he'd come over to check on them as kids, when their dad was sitting in the county jail, sleeping off his latest binge. Sometimes to beat social services over, letting Taylor know they'd be going back into foster care for a bit.

Now, his face was older. Eyes rimmed with shadows. He was well past retirement age now but would probably never give up his badge until someone pried it from him before laying him in a modest wood box.

He was a good one. And a man that she never wanted to disappoint.

"You look great," he said. "All things considered."

"I don't know about that," she replied, folding her legs under her. "Still feels like my body's waiting for a fight. But being home helps."

He nodded slowly, then reached up to scratch the back of his neck. "I've been meaning to come see you since the morning y'all got back, but I figured you all needed space."

"Thanks." She softened. "But I'm glad you came."

He looked at her a moment, like he was seeing her for the first time since she was sixteen and wild-eyed, carrying the weight of the world, trying to keep her sisters together and on the right track. A sister acting as a self-appointed parent. He'd been her savior then, giving her something to look forward to. A goal for just herself, not for anyone else.

"I've always said you were more like a daughter than a deputy to me."

Taylor felt her stomach knot. Here it comes.

"And I hope you know I mean that. Which is why I'm telling you this straight."

She nodded slowly.

"While you've been gone, things kept rolling. Crime didn't stop just because you were not on the team. We had a couple burglaries out in Reed Creek, one missing kid—turned out to be a custody spat—but it rattled folks. We struggled a little. Definitely missed your skills."

He paused.

"And Shane?" Taylor's lips tightened.

"Shane didn't handle it well. Without you, he tried to run the show like he was in Atlanta or something. That kind of energy don't work here."

She nodded once, slowly. "He doesn't understand the people. Never did."

The sheriff leaned forward, elbows on his knees. "That's exactly it. And I'll be honest—I gave him that detective badge because of a favor. His uncle called it in. State Patrol brass. You know how those things go. But I'm beginning to wonder if I did the right thing."

Taylor blinked. "You brought him in as a favor?"

"I did," he said plainly. "And I've regretted it ever since."

She looked away, jaw clenching as anger uncoiled in her belly. "I trained for that job. I stayed when others left. I built trust with this town. The detective position should've been mine."

"I know," he said. "That's on me. I'm really sorry, Taylor."

She didn't want to hate him for it. But it stung. Because

she'd spent nights dreaming about that badge. And he'd handed it to someone who hadn't earned it, someone who'd left the town behind and only came back when he got bored.

"I need to ask you something," she said. "And this stays between us."

"Go ahead."

"Shane told me That *he* came as a favor. He also told me that he was on board because his fiancée was attacked in the city and, after they broke up, he needed out."

The sheriff's eyebrows lifted. "Fiancée?"

Taylor nodded slowly. "Something like that. Said they'd been mugged. I remember because he said it like he was bragging about taking care of the guy, but he seemed to me to still be carrying the trauma."

Dawkins sat back, shaking his head. "Nah. He's never been engaged. Serial dater, from what I heard. Word from my buddy in Gwinnett is that Shane never got serious with anyone. Never put down roots. Really didn't even have friends. Just sort of ... drifted."

Taylor's mind spun. "So he lied."

"He did."

"Twice."

Dawkins didn't reply.

Taylor stared out the window, watching Diesel chase something across the porch.

Why would Shane lie about his reasons for returning? Why make up a fiancé?

What was he really running from?

The silence stretched.

Finally, the sheriff shifted in his seat. "Penner's stepped up since you've been gone. He's talking to people more. Getting out of the office. Folks have even started inviting him to the Wednesday cookouts again."

Taylor cracked a smile. "He hates those."

"Not anymore," Dawkins said. "He's growing. But he's not you."

He stood then, brushing his hat off with one hand.

"I didn't come to pressure you," he said. "But I've got to fill your position if you're not coming back. The town needs someone steady. And they want you."

She stood, too, fingers curling over the edge of the table.

"I'll call you in the morning," she said. "I need to talk to Sam first."

He paused at the door, then reached out and gently cupped her shoulder. "Whatever you decide, I want you to know that I'm proud of you, and of the work you've done for me"

She nodded, a lump forming in her throat.

He tipped his hat. "You be good now."

Then he was gone, boots thudding down the porch steps, truck engine coughing to life.

Taylor stood there long after he left, staring at the badge still hanging by the back door.

A job she'd earned. A title that defined her.

And a lie that changed everything.

Chapter Thirty-Seven

The table was set with quiet ceremony, as if trying to pretend the night was like any other. Silverware gleamed. Wine glasses waited, delicate and thin-rimmed. The napkins were cloth, folded into precise little fans.

It should've felt elegant. Sophisticated.

But seated across from Suki, with Margot propped up between them in a plush dining chair—sweater slipping off one shoulder, her hair in a soft braid thanks to Carmen—it felt more like a truce dinner before a battle no one had declared. This was a celebration dinner, or at least it was supposed to be. It was the first evening that Margot was well enough to get out of bed for dinner.

Suki's posture was perfect, her face expressionless as she used her fork to slice through a filet of salmon crusted with pistachios. Carmen had added rosemary and lemon zest, making it diabetic-friendly and still flavorful.

"This is excellent," Lucy offered, trying to break the quiet.

"Carmen outdid herself," Suki replied, not quite smiling.

Carmen finished setting down a bowl of greens and finally

pulled out a chair of her own, sitting with a soft grunt. "The vinaigrette has olive oil and just a little agave. No sugar," she told Margot gently.

Margot gave a slow nod and stabbed at a tomato like it might talk back. "Looks like it came from a garden that listens to prayers," she murmured.

Suki raised a brow but said nothing.

"I used to have a garden," Margot continued. "Many years ago."

"I have one at my home, on my balcony," Carmen said. "A tiny one made of many colorful pots. I grow the very best cilantro and hot peppers."

Margot smiled at her.

Lucy tucked into her plate, keeping her tone light as she opened a new subject. "Suki, I've been working on that salon showing for Jackie Schafer. It's in the early stages, but she's interested."

Carmen paused mid-bite. "Jackie Schafer? The one who talks like she's above the air she breathes?"

Lucy smiled faintly. "That's the one."

Suki's expression sharpened with interest. She played along. "Smart choice. She moves in strategic circles. If you get her attention, you'll get the attention of everyone."

"I'm hoping to introduce new blood. I've got an artist I'm bringing in—Leena Raines." Lucy pulled up the photo of the art piece on her phone, holding it out for a quick glance.

A vivid, daring self-portrait blurred in reds and black. It still nearly caught her breath.

Suki nodded. "Nice. Has she sold anything yet?"

"I don't think so," Lucy replied. "She needs representation."

"Then she's raw," Suki said. "And hungry. You can work with that."

An image of Jorge filled Lucy's mind. He'd been raw and hungry. And now his work was selling for prices he never dreamed of.

Carmen sat back and resumed her meal. She didn't ask questions, but Lucy caught the subtle lift of her eyebrow. Suspicious, but silent.

Lucy slid the phone back into her pocket and powered it off.

"I'm actually going to let Jackie have her, if all works out," Lucy said.

"Good move," Suki nearly purred.

Margot's voice came soft from the end of the table, interrupting with her own interests, looking at Lucy. "You remember Mike? The guitar guy with the old harmonica?"

Lucy blinked at the sudden shift. "Of course I do. I saw him a few days ago when I had the dogs at the park."

"He could make a cardboard box sound like a lullaby," Margot said dreamily. "And Armina. I wonder if she still carries her baby everywhere?"

"I assume she does," Lucy said, her voice quieting.

Margot frowned. "I know they're not getting what they need out there. Not in this heat. It's like breathing soup."

"I'll take a case of electrolyte water," Lucy said. "Tomorrow morning. I'll find one of your old friends to share it with the others."

"I want to come." Margot looked like an eager child, her fork mid-air to her mouth.

Lucy and Carmen spoke at the same time: "No."

She sagged a little in her seat, shoulders drooping. "But I'm better."

"You're not strong enough for that yet," Carmen said gently. "It would take everything out of you to go down to the park and walk around. You'd be set back too far."

"I know," Margot sighed. "But I just miss them."

"We'll tell them you're asking," Lucy promised. Margot was like a mother hen, worried for her chicks. "And I'll bring a picture of you. Let them see how much better you are. I'll take it when we finish eating."

That got a small smile out of Margot. "Take them something sweet, too, with the water. Something soft. Some of them can't chew so well."

"I'll pick up donuts," Lucy promised.

Dinner moved along slowly after that. Polite. Muted. The kind of meal where everyone was careful with their words. If Suki hadn't been with them, there would've been a lightness. Some laughter.

Her serious countenance was like a blanket smothering a flame.

When Carmen stacked the dishes and the plates were cleared, Suki dabbed her mouth with her napkin and stood. "Come with me, Lucia. Let's find you something unforgettable to wear for Jackie's little gathering."

Lucy rose, smoothing her skirt, but paused to glance at Margot.

Carmen moved to her side with a hand out. "I'll help you to the couch. You can watch something in here tonight."

Margot looked after Suki, then shook her head. "Just help me to my room. I'm tired."

Their eyes met.

Something unspoken passed between them. Something old. Something feral and warning.

Lucy swallowed. "I'll check on you in a bit," she said. "And take that photo."

Carmen led Margot gently away, murmuring something soft in Spanish. Lucy turned toward Suki, who had already started walking down the hallway like she expected to be followed.

Every Little Thing

And she would be.

But Lucy's steps felt heavier now.

Her mind was already tracing the edges of the truth she hadn't yet admitted—about Ian's old files. The list of stolen works tucked in her blouse, now hidden inside her toiletry bag under the sink, had confirmed what she feared. Art theft. More laundering. Pieces sent to Ukraine under the guise of "family acquisitions."

And now she had a name.

A Ukrainian surname. A shipping address. And leverage, if she ever needed it.

But that knowledge sat like a hot coal in her chest—burning quietly, reminding her how close to the fire she already was.

She eased herself down onto Suki's bed, feeling the weight of the world on her shoulders. What should she do with everything she knows now?

"If you have to sit, could you use the chair over there, please?" Suki asked, gesturing to an armchair in the corner. "That's a ten-thousand-dollar bed when you consider it's from Europe and is fit with Frette sheets and coverings."

Lucy moved to the chair. She couldn't care less what kind of bed or bedding it was. Ten thousand dollars could go a long way in doing something good for people, instead of used to pamper an already spoiled socialite.

Suki opened the door to her walk-in closet and gestured grandly. "Pick anything. I want Jackie to regret not buying it first."

Lucy stepped inside. Silks and velvets lined the walls. Labels like Givenchy, Dior, McQueen. But as her fingers brushed along a row of hangers, her thoughts were still with Margot.

Was she picking up on something Lucy wasn't?

Was her hesitation tonight just fatigue—or instinct?

Lucy tried to push it down, tried to focus on textures, cuts, necklines.

But as she stepped into the closet's soft, perfumed hush, one thought came sharp and unrelenting:

You're already in too far. And you don't even know how deep the water goes yet.

Chapter Thirty-Eight

The cart squeaked like it had a guilty conscience. Lucy tugged it gently over the cobblestones near the park's west entrance, where tourists in wide-brimmed hats and clunky sandals pointed toward the skyline, phones raised like shields. Beside her, Carmen walked with purposeful strides, her expression unreadable behind dark sunglasses.

The cart was stacked: hand fans, batteries, wet wipes, several cases of bottled water, and a full bushel of oranges. Atop it all, delicately balanced, sat a flat cardboard box wrapped in twine—Margot's promised offering of donuts.

The city was already sweltering by late morning. Pigeons flapped and cooed around the benches, their wings fanning up dust. A saxophonist played somewhere down the path, his sound weaving through the air like warm smoke. Vendors called out over the noise, hawking churros, balloons, caricature sketches, hot dogs. Central Park had its usual sheen of wonder and wealth, but Lucy could already feel the edges—the places most people didn't see.

She remembered how to find them.

Mike found her first.

He appeared beside a tree, guitar slung over his shoulder by a canvas strap, his eyes shadowed by a camo ball cap that might have been green once. His beard was a wiry mess of gray, but his back was still straight. Proud. His eyes flicked to the cart, then to Lucy.

"Well, I'll be damned," he said, squinting. "I remember you. It's been a few years though."

Lucy stopped. "Hey, Mike. You're the man we're looking for."

He crossed his arms. "What was it—four nights you lasted out here before jumping ship to the big house? From the streets to The Dakota, I believe, if I'm not mistaken."

She winced, then nodded. "Something like that."

The accusation wasn't cruel. Just honest.

Carmen stepped in, her voice light. "Margot sent reinforcements, and her love."

Mike's mouth twitched, and he nodded once. "Now, that woman ... she lasted. Is she with you?"

Lucy nodded. "Yes, she's across the street now too. Getting better every day." She showed him the photo and Mike brushed tears from his eyes as he turned away. He motioned them to follow and led them off the beaten path, away from the joggers and yogis and vendors. Deeper into the belly of the park.

Past a line of hedges, through a narrow dirt cut-through, they arrived at what looked like a makeshift village packed into the narrow space between a low retaining wall and a stand of tall shrubs. Blankets, tarps, a few rolling suitcases. Milk crates for chairs. A blue tarp had been strung between two trees to provide shade.

And they were there. A dozen familiar faces, some aged, some broken.

And Armina.

She was sitting cross-legged on a wool blanket, her doll

nestled in her lap, wrapped in a pink baby onesie. She looked pale, and thinner, it seemed, from the brief encounter when Lucy first returned to the city. The wrinkles and grooves lined her face, making deep paths between all the sun damage she wore like a badge of bravery. She rocked her baby gently, humming a lullaby Lucy remembered from her first nights in the park.

"Dormi, dormi, bel bambino..."

When Armina saw Lucy, she stopped rocking. Her eyes, though glassy, lit up with something fragile and sweet, like a child on Christmas morning, full of hope for the best gifts.

Carmen and Mike began handing out supplies. Fans were snapped open, passed hand to hand. Water bottles were cracked and shared immediately. The box of donuts made the rounds like treasure.

Lucy knelt beside Armina, pulled the phone from her coat pocket, and held it out. Margot, smiling faintly in bed, braid over one shoulder, eyes clearer than they'd been in years.

Armina clapped softly with her fingertips. "Bella, bella Margot," she whispered, tears pricking her lashes. "I need her. My chosen sister, Margot."

One of the women beside her gasped when she saw it, then began to cry openly. Another man said a prayer, his hand pressed to his chest.

Mike stood off to the side, his arms folded. He didn't dare look at it again.

"She's doing better," Lucy said. "She asked me to bring you the news. And the donuts."

There was laughter, soft and unexpected.

"She's our matriarch," Mike said gruffly. "Always shared everything she had. I seen her wash people's feet with her last bit of water when the park's system was shut down for a week."

Lucy nodded, throat tight.

That's when she saw Armina's ankle.

Blood streaked her heel, trailing down from a wound swollen and red. A small piece of cardboard had been tied around it like a bandage.

Carmen appeared beside her before Lucy could call out.

"First aid kit," she said, already pulling gloves from the zip pouch she'd strapped to the cart.

Armina let her do it without protest, humming all the while. Carmen took her shoes off and poured clean water over the wound, wiped it gently, applied ointment, and pressed a fresh bandage down. Then she looked at the sandals that had graced Armina's feet—frayed, shredded, toe seams gone—and shook her head.

She stood up, stepped out of her own sandals, and knelt to help Armina into them.

"They'll fit you better anyway," she said.

Lucy looked away, blinking fast.

Armina giggled in delight.

"You don't need to fuss like this," Mike muttered. But his voice cracked just slightly. "I've got it handled." He glanced at Armina, his expression one of pity and concern.

Lucy stepped close to him, lowered her voice. "It's not fuss. It's thanks."

He didn't answer, but, after a beat, he nodded once, his chin dropping toward his chest.

The rest of the visit passed in quiet moments—one woman reciting a poem she'd written, another man offering Carmen a carved bead. They didn't ask for anything else. Just thanked them, one by one.

Lucy took the opportunity to ask Mike if he knew anyone who would do a direct trade of her Jeep for a van. He gave her an address of someone he trusted.

As they turned to leave, Mike raised a hand.

"Tell her thanks," he said, then his voice got even more gravelly. "And—and tell her we miss her."

Lucy nodded, overwhelmed.

They didn't talk on the walk back. Carmen pulled the empty cart with slow, barefoot steps, her expression unreadable.

Lucy walked beside her, the image of Armina cradling her doll burned into her mind.

And Margot's soft voice, somewhere in the distance of her memory. Words from the first time she knew her: *Don't forget who you were, baby. That's how you remember who you want to be.*

Chapter Thirty-Nine

Lucy took a long, worried breath and steeled herself for the next part of the evening. The last of the guests floated out like perfume on silk, leaving Jackie's spectacular apartment bathed in candlelight and low music. Empty champagne flutes dotted the bar, a plate of forgotten figs sat half-eaten on the edge of a coffee table. The night had shimmered with potential, and not just because of Leena Raines' work—though the pieces Lucy had curated had stirred plenty of murmurs. Leena's raw edges and feral femininity were noted, even praised.

No bids on anything, but it was enough that Jackie was going to offer representation to Leena.

But nothing drew gasps like the piece of the night: *Doll in Velvet*. Jackie's prized painting. The one Lucy had come to steal.

Jackie stood at the center of it all, poised and elegant, thanking guests with practiced charm. Her hair was untouched by the humidity, her voice low and commanding. She moved through her home like a hostess queen—and every glance she cast Lucy's way reminded her this night was about her, and her ability to discover a new artist. Even if technically, Lucy was the one who'd brought Leena to her.

Lucy lingered near the hallway, waiting for the room to completely clear so she could speak privately to Jackie. So she could put into play her next moves. Her fingers curled tight around her champagne glass. She felt the moment building, her nerves humming. But then—

The elevator dinged.

She glanced up, pulse hitching. He stepped out with sense of purpose. Jorge.

His dark hair, brushed back to reveal those impossible cheekbones. His white, pristine shirt open at the collar. No tie. Well-fitting black trousers, emphasizing every muscle and making Lucy remember exactly how he looked without them.

His presence shook something loose inside her, the part of her that had been frozen for far too long. She immediately turned and began to retreat into the next room.

"Lucia," Jackie called out, eyes glinting. "Don't you dare run. Come back."

Lucy hesitated in the doorway.

Jackie crossed the room to meet her, the click of her heels sharp against the polished floor. "He's a friend of mine and I invited him," she said softly. "After the last party, he pulled me aside and told me everything. What he felt for you. What he still feels."

"Jackie—" Lucy began.

But Jackie cut her off. "You can avoid your fate once. But if you let it pass you by again, when it comes to love? Now that's a crime."

Her last word was ironic, considering Suki's commands for later.

Jackie gently turned Lucy back around and gave her a soft push.

Jorge waited by the window, a wine glass in his hand and his eyes trained on the skyline. When he turned and saw her, his whole face shifted—something unguarded broke through. Vulnerable. Raw.

"Lucia," he said.

"Jorge," she whispered.

Neither of them moved for a moment. The silence stretched between them, not awkward, but heavy with everything left unsaid.

"I'm sorry," she said finally, her voice cracking. "For disappearing. For not calling. For—everything."

He shook his head slowly. "You think I didn't know where you were?"

She blinked.

"You weren't difficult to track once you sold your first piece, but I didn't follow. Didn't reach out. I didn't want to barge in where I wasn't wanted."

"You were wanted," she said quietly. "I—"

"But not enough," he said, a flicker of pain cutting through the softness in his voice. "I thought maybe you'd found someone better."

"I did try," she admitted, thinking of Shane Weaver, and a handful of other guys she'd dated. Guys whose names she couldn't even recall. Just filler for the lonely ache in her heart. "But it never worked out because I couldn't stop thinking about you."

He stepped closer and put his hand on her arm. "I still live in the same place. We can talk. Please, Lucia."

His touch made her body instantly feel hot as fire. She closed her eyes. Meeting him alone wasn't a good idea. She wouldn't be able to resist him, only to have to leave him again. She didn't want to hurt him again. "I don't think I can."

He touched her arm gently, then lifted his hand to her lips and pressed a finger there before leaning in next to her ear.

"Shh," he whispered, the warm air and his lips sending a chill through her. "Midnight. I'll be waiting."

And just like that, he was gone.

Lucy stood frozen for a long moment before she turned back to Jackie, who was already watching her with a smirk and a half-raised brow.

Jackie lifted her glass. "We both figured out who you are and where you're from. So … do you want to tell me what's really going on, or are we still playing 'Lucia Leighton the Magnificent?'"

Lucy exhaled shakily. This was what she'd been waiting for. An opening. "Yes, I want to tell you the truth. All of it. I'm here for another motive. One that is quite nefarious."

Jackie didn't look surprised. "Knew it. Come sit down. We're going to need some more wine for this, I can feel it."

They sat by her display wall, candlelight catching the edge of *Doll in Velvet*, the centerpiece of the night. A nice crisp Riesling cooling in their glasses.

Lucy began to speak, voice low and careful as she started at the beginning. She told Jackie how she came to meet Ian, her original homeless-to-dog-walker status. Then the promotion to becoming his protégé. The transformation to Lucia Leighton, from a fine family on Martha's Vineyard.

She chronicled Ian's manipulation. Suki's fake identity as his wife. The art laundering she discovered.

The child they tried to buy from her.

Barely taking a breath between, she moved on to her escape. The fear. How Suki nearly double-crossed her. When she told her of fleeing, of taking her baby back to Georgia, to the farm and the quaint cabin for her and Johnny, her voice shook. Describing the animal rescue made her proud of her family and what they were doing for the community, and the successful dog-boarding business that helped fund it was another feather in her cap.

She told of how happy she was when she'd discovered Faire's art and that she could make something of herself, finally. How maybe Johnny never needed to know how far she'd once fallen, living on the streets, the drugs and boozing. Meeting his father, and being his mistress, nearly taking a father from his wife and children.

She paused, trembling as she struggled with the shame of the life she'd lived, heat filling her face. She jumped back to safer things—her family. Her sisters, especially Taylor who had always been there for them and done the right thing in every circumstance. Anna, once in a terrible marriage but slowly rebuilding a solid career and new life for herself and her kids.

Cate and how she'd been taken from them when they were kids, leaving them with an alcoholic father, jumping in and out of foster care.

Of Jo, and the betrayal and near tragedy she brought to them. How, like Lucy, Jo fought her internal demons of a childhood without a mother, and making too many mistakes as an adult. But how, despite everything, she was a wonderful mother to her son, Levi, who was growing up to be a good human being despite not having a father.

How they couldn't seem to escape trauma in their lives, like a cloud followed them from year to year, drifting down just when they thought they'd overcome the worst of it.

"But look," Jackie interjected. "It sounds like all of you are overcoming it as it comes." Her pristine exterior was beginning to crack, like lacquer peeling from aged wood, showing the layers of empathy and compassion beneath. Sides of herself that most had never seen.

Then Lucy spoke of the voices. The paranoia and how she

wasn't quite sure if it was all in her head, or if Ian's family was still watching her, waiting for a moment to swoop in and take Johnny from her—the only thing in the world she cared about.

"Can I see a photo of your son?" Jackie interrupted.

Lucy pulled out her phone and found some of the most recent. Johnny with his towhead and blue eyes, grinning up at the camera as he held a small garden snake out. Him with his cousins, Levi and Teague, fishing off the dock. Then he and Lucy, snuggled together in her bed, taking selfies to make him giggle.

"He's beautiful," Jackie whispered. "Absolutely gorgeous. I can see you in him, Lucia."

"Thank you," Lucy said, and continued her story, telling about running away from him, from home and all those dear to her, from the sanctuary she'd found and that was now a place of worry. A place that had brought her huge anxiety.

"Dear girl," Jackie said. "I hate to ask, but are you on medication?"

"Yes, I am now. And I'm better. Truly. But Suki led me to believe that perhaps her family really is holding a grudge. Perhaps they do want Johnny, even though he wasn't really Ian's child. Maybe it's not all misplaced paranoia."

"I'm not sure that makes sense," Jackie said, her expression doubting.

Lucy threw her hands up. "Nothing makes sense to me right now. All I know is that Suki has a hold on me, and, to be free from her and her family, I had to agree to do one thing. She promised safety—but— (she hesitated) ... only if I stole *Doll in Velvet*."

Jackie was taken aback for a few seconds before she guffawed harshly, as though the thought was laughable. She stood, put aside her wine and poured herself a fresh whiskey—neat, no ice.

"Before we get to that, I have to say that it's very convenient that Ian's dead. That Suki, your partner in crime, will benefit from this little escapade. And maybe you too. Tell me, Lucia—or should I say Lucy—did you kill him?'

"No," Lucy exclaimed, horrified. "I never touched him. I believe it was Suki. She called him to pick her up when we were together that last night. Then he ended up dead the same night. It's too coincidental. She hated him with a vengeance too. Ian and their father kept Suki from being with the man she loved, and he married someone else. They forced her into pretending to be Ian's wife. She was miserable until he was dead."

"And dear Suki thinks stealing my centerpiece will elevate her clout to that her brother had earned here in this crazy city of competitiveness?"

Lucy nodded. "She believes she deserves it."

"And you were going to take it?"

"I was supposed to. But I'm not."

Jackie stared at her. "Then what are you doing?"

"I'm going to make her believe I did. Long enough to get my friend Margot out of her house before Suki throws her to the curb."

Jackie's brow lifted. "And you need me?"

"A van. Quiet. Discreet. Big enough for a hospital bed. And I know this is a lot to ask, but I need that painting. Just for a few nights and, I swear, you'll get it back."

Jackie sipped her whiskey. "And what do I get in return?"

"The satisfaction of knowing you outplayed Ian from beyond the grave. And Suki in the flesh."

A long pause. Then Jackie nodded slowly.

"That's tempting."

"If it works out the way I plan, Suki and her family in Ukraine will be so busy fighting extradition that they won't ever think of me again."

"You better pull this off," Jackie said, voice sharp. "Because, if this goes sideways, I'll pretend you were in on the theft. Your name will be erased from my mind and my clients after you are prosecuted. And I'll make sure every gallery from here to Berlin does the same."

Lucy offered a small smile. "Fair enough."

Jackie stood and called for her assistant. "Let's arrange your getaway vehicle. Quietly. And, if you see Jorge again ..." She paused. "Don't be stupid. That man still looks at you like he's painting you in his head."

Lucy turned away, trying not to let her heart splinter at the sound of his name.

———

Lucy told herself she was just walking. Just one loop around the block. Just one more glance at the building's old red-brick façade with its soot-lined windows and chipped stoop. The third time around, she nearly convinced herself she was just pacing off nerves. That the fluttering in her chest was from adrenaline, not want.

But, on the fourth pass, she looked up.

And there he was.

Jorge, silhouetted by the soft amber light of his apartment window, one hand resting on the frame, watching her like he knew she'd show up all along. He didn't wave. He didn't move.

He just watched.

Lucy stopped breathing. Her feet stopped moving. A cab honked behind her and rolled by, but she didn't notice. She lifted her hand, barely, and gave the smallest of nods.

The window light disappeared.

She climbed the stairs without thinking. Her fingers shook

as she pressed the buzzer, but, before she could let go, the door clicked.

Inside, nothing had changed.

Same creaky third step on the staircase. Same hallway smell of old wood, paint, and someone's forgotten laundry. And when Jorge opened the door to his apartment, it was still the same shoebox she remembered—too small for his talent, too humble for the kind of money his name now brought in.

But it was warm. And clean. And it was his.

"I didn't think you'd come," he said softly.

Lucy stepped in, heart in her throat. "I didn't think I would either."

He closed the door behind her and leaned back against it, arms crossed. He looked at her like she was both a wound and the salve for it.

"You still live here," she said, "Why?"

He shrugged. "I thought if you ever came back, this is where you'd look for me first."

Lucy laughed, but it cracked halfway out.

He motioned her in and walked toward the back where several canvases leaned against the wall. "You want to see what I've been working on?"

She nodded and followed.

There were fewer pieces than she expected. Half-finished abstracts. Quiet studies of faces without eyes. A piece with brushstrokes like fingerprints in cobalt and wine red.

"They're ... different," she said.

"I don't paint for money anymore," he said. "Only for peace. But it's hard to find when your heart's still mostly empty."

She turned to him slowly. "Jorge ..."

He held her gaze for a long time. Then sat on the edge of his worn gray couch and patted the cushion beside him. "Talk to me."

So she did.

"My name is not Lucia," she started. Then she told him everything. About her life on the streets of New York. About Ian, about the art. The fake persona. Johnny. Her family. Suki. The painting. The danger. The darkness. She spoke until her voice went hoarse, and her hands were fists in her lap. He listened. Never once interrupted. Never once looked away.

When she finished, she waited for him to recoil. To judge. To push her out the door.

Instead, he reached for her hands and gently unfurled them.

"I also have secrets," he began. "Damage from my childhood. I've been reading a book that explores the possibility of inherited trauma. I do believe that a lot of the battles we go through, the emotional and mental pain, the wrong paths, can be attributed to battles fought from those who come before us. Our DNA is passed down from the family tree of so many ghosts who shape what we are born with. Our parents, grandparents, and even further back. We are born into this world carrying invisible particles of pain and survival from our ancestors."

Lucy thought about Cate, and her battles with her parents, then the abuse she suffered from their dad. The fire. The decades in prison with everything she'd gone through to survive it.

Adele. Her grandmother surely carried some sort of emotional pain. That was evident in the closed off way she interacted with the world. Possibly something from her own childhood or her marriage.

The idea of inherited trauma sort of made sense to Lucy. Was her journey the aftermath of those who came before her, too? Was her own rebellious streak that sent her on such a rocky path given to her from the echoes of the past?

Tears blurred her vision, but she didn't let them fall. She

stared at their joined hands. "I've done so many terrible things. You just can't imagine."

"And I've done selfish ones," he said. "Walked away from people. Took commissions from men I knew were laundering money through my work. We all fall. But failing and falling isn't the end unless you let it be. I've also discovered this too. Life isn't about who you once were," he said. "It's about who you are now, and who you have the potential to be, if you want it bad enough."

She didn't know what to say.

"Lucy, I've bought land in Uruguay," he continued. "An orchard. Olives, citrus, figs. It's a mess but, somehow, despite the neglect, the fruit still blooms. The place needs everything. But it's mine. And it's quiet there and so private. The air smells like earth and firewood. At night, you can see every star in the sky. It has every little thing a person could ever need, and nothing they don't."

She closed her eyes, imagining it. A place without chaos. A simple place Johnny could run barefoot in the grass. A place without Ian's ghost or her memories, and where a couple could build upon their dreams.

"There's a house too," Jorge added. "It's crumbling, but it has promise. Like you."

She looked at him then, and he moved closer.

"The only finished room there is my art studio, and I sleep there, where I don't feel so alone."

Before she realized it, they were sitting on the edge of the bed. It wasn't just a mattress on the floor anymore—he'd bought a frame at some point—but it still creaked with memory.

His fingers found her wrist first, then slid up her arm like he was learning her again.

"I shouldn't—" she began.

He placed a finger against her lips. "Shhh, *Cariño mío*. Let's talk with our bodies, not our voices. I have missed the way you talk to me that way. I've missed every little thing about you."

His lips met hers, and the world went quiet as he lay her back, his arm cradling her descent. She remembered the smell of him—spicy and warm, like sandalwood and sun—and she breathed it in deeply, so deep it would stay with her forever. His hands were familiar and new all at once. She let herself fall, not into danger or pretense, but into the one place she hadn't allowed herself to go for such a long time. And she wouldn't apologize for it either.

At least, for now.

Chapter Forty

The sun was just beginning to light the edges of Manhattan's skyline when Lucy stepped out of the Uber and onto the curb in front of Suki's building. The sky above was a pink wash of early light, the streets still mostly quiet, but the adrenaline in her blood was louder than the morning.

She wore black from head to toe—leggings, soft cotton tee, zip-up hoodie, and sleek sneakers. Her hair was pulled into a low twist, and her eyes still carried shadows, though not from exhaustion. No, the night with Jorge had left her glowing in places she hadn't realized were starved. She could still feel his fingertips on her spine, the murmur of his breath against her ear.

But that was then. She needed to leave that behind for the performance of a lifetime.

The doorman barely gave her a glance. Upstairs, the elevator opened with a soft chime—and Suki was already waiting.

Hands on hips. Silk robe belted tight. Expression carved from ice and accusation.

"Where the hell have you been?" she hissed.

Lucy barely blinked. "I told you. I had to wait until Jackie was good and asleep. She told me she has insomnia and doesn't drift off until the wee hours." She stepped past her, letting the weight of the oversized black canvas bag shift in her grip.

"Who were you waiting with?" Suki demanded, following like a shark that smelled a drop of betrayal.

"Jorge."

Suki stilled. "Jorge Vanzo?"

"I saw him at the party. He ... asked me to come over."

Suki narrowed her eyes. "I didn't realize you two were on those terms again."

"We weren't. Now we are."

"Convenient," Suki muttered.

"Don't worry, he has no idea what I was up to when I left him." Lucy moved into the office and dropped the bag onto the floor with a grunt. She pulled her gloves from her pocket and slipped them on. The moment stretched as she unzipped the bag slowly. Carefully.

Inside, wrapped in a thick layer of black velvet and archival bubble wrap, was *Doll in Velvet*—Jackie Schafer's coveted masterpiece.

Lucy pulled the fabric back like she was unveiling a religious artifact.

Suki's breath caught.

She was on it in seconds.

"Oh my God," she whispered, crouching to her knees in front of it. "Oh my God, this is it. This is really it." She reached forward and placed both hands on the edge of the canvas.

Lucy watched, her stomach twisting.

Suki's fingers ran lightly over the thick, luscious strokes of oil paint, her mouth slightly open.

"Holy shit, you did it," she said, laughing, euphoric. "I mean, you really did it. But how? I want every detail how you pulled this off. Oh, if I could just see her face when she realizes it's gone."

Lucy spun her story of lies like silk. "I waited until the apartment was dark. Slipped back in through the side service entrance. Jackie leaves it unlocked sometimes—bad habit. I shut down the hallway security panel and used a backup code I found written in her office drawer last night while she was schmoozing guests."

Suki grinned, wicked. "What an idiot. Who writes down their security code?" She traced a nail along the edge of the frame. "This is going to be priceless in a few more years. When the public thinks it's gone forever, when demand swells. My father is going to—" She stopped.

Lucy froze.

Suki was still looking at the painting, caressing it like a prize show horse. "He's going to lose his mind when he sees what I'm sending home. Then he'll finally realize I'm just as good as Ian."

The words were acid.

Lucy's spine went cold. "You said you cut ties with your father."

Suki barely blinked. "Did I? Maybe I said I was trying. Or maybe you just heard what you wanted."

A long pause. Then Suki smirked, brushing her hair back from her face. "Don't look so shocked, Lucia. You know better than that. They'll never let me be free."

Lucy didn't reply. She bent down, folding the velvet back over the canvas with reverence. Her gloves were still on.

"You don't trust me now?" Suki asked, teasing.

Lucy had suspected that Suki wasn't living her own life. That she was still connected. But the confirmation made her feel sick.

She gave her a smile so thin it might as well have been a blade. "Of course I do."

Every Little Thing

Suki stood. "I'm going to shower and nap. I barely slept waiting for you." She yawned, already halfway to the bedroom. "I want to enjoy it for a few days before we get it ready for the courier. Oh, and dear Lucia, thank you for being my partner in crime. Now I know you'll never double-cross me like you did my brother."

She disappeared.

Lucy didn't move for a long minute.

The silence closed in. The painting stared up at her, waiting.

It was over. The mask had dropped. Suki was never going to stop being dangerous.

She hadn't turned on her family. She'd just lied better than Ian ever did.

Lucy stood slowly, peeled off the gloves, and walked out of the office. Her heart was thundering now—not with fear, but resolve. She needed to make a call tonight.

Another proposition. One that would decide the rest of her life.

She stepped into her room, shut the door quietly, and turned on the lamp. She stared at the ceiling, tears threatening but not quite falling.

"Soon, baby," she whispered, eyes fluttering closed. "I'm coming home to you soon."

To Johnny. To Hart's Ridge. To the farm and the rescue and the fields. Miles of country roads with nothing but scenery. Streets barely peppered with pedestrians. No chaos. No noise.

She was going to buy back her soul with this.

And pray to God it was enough.

Chapter Forty-One

She woke with a jolt, heart already thudding. Three days. That's how long it had taken to plan the escape. Three days of news briefs about a stolen painting from one of New York's leading art collectors. Three days of pretending everything was fine. Three days of Suki basking in the glow of her stolen prize, wandering the penthouse in silk robes, sipping wine, laughing at the news briefs and dreaming aloud of the painting's journey back to Ukraine— "with the perfect silent message to my father," she'd said smugly more than once.

Lucy had smiled and nodded. Waited nervously. What if Jackie turned on her?

Now, the time had come. The painting was finally packed up, sitting in Ian's office, the courier scheduled to come pick it up in the morning. It was now or never.

Her phone buzzed once with a text from Carmen.

Ready.

Lucy slipped from bed and into the soft black clothes she'd laid out the night before. She didn't bother brushing her hair.

Pulled it into a loose tie at the nape of her neck. She grabbed her small duffel, packed only with the things she'd brought from Georgia. She refused to take anything bought with Suki's money. That chapter was over, and those clothes and shoes held bad energy.

She eased open the bedroom door. Carmen stood at the end of the hallway in dark jeans, a hoodie, and silent sneakers. She nodded once, then turned, vanishing into the maid's corridor where Lucy followed.

Together, they entered Margot's room.

The older woman stirred as Lucy knelt beside her. "It's time, love," she whispered. "We are done with our stay here."

Margot blinked, confused, but smiled weakly. "Where are we going?"

"We'll tell you in the van," Carmen murmured as she helped pull the blanket away. "Just trust me."

"I always have," Margot rasped.

Lucy and Carmen helped her sit up, dress slowly. Carmen wrapped a scarf gently around her neck, then added a cardigan despite the early summer heat. "For the ride," she said softly. "In case the air conditioning is chilly for you."

When Margot was ready, Lucy slipped into the hall to retrieve the last of the bags, and Carmen darted away to fetch the dogs.

Moments later, Ginger and Bentley padded softly down the hallway. Lucy put Bentley on a leash just in case he decided to wander. Ginger was alert and eager, obediently walking with Lucy, tail wagging fast, like she could sense the tension. Bentley, in his usual state of mild disinterest, gave a sniff and trotted ahead as far as the leash would allow.

With bags slung over their shoulders and the sound of Margot's breath rattling between them, they moved down the back halls, silent as ghosts.

The service elevator waited. Lucy hit the button. Her heart thundered.

Ding.

It sounded loud as thunder in the deserted hall.

They stepped in. Carmen kept her arm tight around Margot's waist, while Lucy handled the dogs and the food Carmen had packed—juice, glucose tabs, bananas, a container filled with peanut butter sandwiches, and enough bottled water. She had thought of everything.

The elevator opened at the loading bay—cold concrete and fluorescent lights.

Edward was already there. He looked at his watch, then tipped his cap. "Right on time. Security system reboot started twenty-two minutes ago. You've got eight minutes. After that, everything's back online."

Lucy nodded. "Thank you."

Suki would never know that Carmen helped them.

"My pleasure. I never have liked that woman," he muttered. He didn't know all the details of what was going down, but he knew enough to know that Suki wasn't going to be happy at the nighttime exodus.

He was going to get a huge surprise in just a few minutes. And the next morning, when he went to his station, he'd find a note and the keys to her Jeep, along with the name of the parking deck where it was parked. She'd already put his name on the back of the title.

A thank you for all his kindness.

The discreet van Jackie had arranged idled by the far door. It was matte gray, windows blacked out. Lucy opened the side doors.

Inside, the hospital bed was secured with straps, cushioned with pillows and thick blankets. A small oxygen tank, water bottles, and first aid supplies were strapped to the wall.

Sitting in the seat set up next to the bed was Armina.

She wore her signature black and gold Versace scarf and held her doll cradled in one arm. Carmen's sandals still on her feet. Her eyes lit up when she saw Margot.

"Little bird," she said dreamily. "We're going on a journey."

"Yes," Lucy whispered, helping Margot up the small ramp with Carmen's aid. "We are."

Carmen gave Margot one last blanket, tucked it up to her chin.

Margot smiled. "You're both angels."

Lucy turned to Carmen, eyes stinging. "Promise me you'll come to Georgia. You won't have to put up with being a servant to anyone else again. Lot of jobs there where you can be your own person. You'll come?"

"I will. I've got family to think of too. We can't vanish the same night as you. Suki will know."

Lucy hated to leave her. "Okay, but call me when it's safe. I'll have a place ready for you and your family until you get your feet on the ground."

They embraced, tight and silent.

Carmen bent and kissed Margot's forehead. "Stay alive, old woman." She whispered something else in Spanish and crossed her chest in a catholic prayer.

Margot grinned. "You always were too bossy."

Carmen gave Armina a soft pat on the shoulder. "You take care of yourself."

Armina nodded solemnly. "I always do."

Lucy was happy that, now, Armina would have help doing it.

She climbed into the driver's seat, heart racing, and started the van. Carmen shut the doors, a final bang that echoed in the concrete cavern.

They eased out of The Dakota property, rolling to the edge

of the street with Lucy's hands trembling on the steering wheel, her stomach in her throat.

They turned left at the end of the block, and she stopped in front of the early morning coffee vendor. Someone walked out from the shadows and the passenger door opened.

Jorge threw his duffel bag into the back and swung into the passenger seat. His grin under the dome light was so bright, despite her nervousness, Lucy couldn't help but smile back.

"Nice timing," she said, glad he'd taken her up on her proposition.

He looked her over. "Like I could ever say no to you, my love. And you're in black again. Very dramatic. I like it."

She eyed his flannel shirt and scuffed boots. He'd dropped the brooding artist persona. "Well, I see you're dressing for Georgia country already."

He winked. "I plan to fully embrace the lifestyle and can't wait to leave this cesspool of a city."

Then—sirens.

Lucy's body snapped straight. She whipped her head toward the mirror.

Blue and red lights flooded through the street behind them, turning toward The Dakota building.

"C'mon, Lucia. Let's get out of here," Jorge said.

Lucy gripped the steering wheel as they peeled around the corner, van humming low and smooth. She twisted in her seat, just enough to catch one last glimpse of what she was leaving behind.

Suki. Her penthouse. Both cold and cavernous and full of lies.

She whispered, "She'll never sleep in that ten-thousand-dollar bed again."

Not tonight.

Not for a long, long time.

EPILOGUE

Home wasn't just a place. It was a feeling stitched into the seams of every quiet moment where one felt safe. The swing on Taylor's porch creaked gently beneath Armina, its chain groaning in the lazy rhythm of August heat. Armina sat cross-legged, cradling her baby, humming a lullaby in Italian. Her doll was dressed in a crisp old-fashioned pinafore dress and tiny button-up black satin slippers. Clothes bought by Cate, an assortment of choices she'd found in an antique store, knowing the woman would treasure being able to dress her doll up.

Armina wore a clean floral blouse Lucy had found at a thrift store, and still donned the black and gold Versace scarf, now pressed and pinned just right.

Lucy breathed in deeply, all the way down to her lungs and then her soul. The air smelled like honeysuckle and grass. Cicadas hummed somewhere in the trees. The sun had begun its slow descent over the tree line, brushing everything in gold—fields, porch rails, dog fur, and the crown of Lucy's head as it leaned against Jorge's shoulder. She'd gone back to her natural color, upon Jorge's request, but it made her feel like herself again too.

EPILOGUE

On the far end of the porch, Margot reclined in a lawn chair with a library paperback open across her lap. Once she'd been fitted with eyeglasses, she'd discovered she loved reading. Big, thick novels too. Not quick and easy books and she wouldn't even entertain the idea of reading on a tablet that would be easier for her hands to hold. No, she wanted the real thing. Her favorite outings were to the library where she no longer had to huddle there for warmth and avoid pitying looks but was now treated as a true and respectable patron—a library card in her hand with a real address.

Her hair, now cropped into a soft bob, was shiny and clean, with silver streaks that shimmered in the light. Bentley had decided that Margot would be his new person, and he sat at her feet, panting with his tongue out.

Margot looked like a woman reborn, so many years of hardship erased from her face.

At her feet lay Ginger—the original Ginger—sprawled and content.

Armina and Margot had taken over Lucy's old cabin. The family had met and decided that, until the ladies were physically unable, they would live out their years there at the farm.

They'd been affectionately termed the family's Golden Girls.

Cate was helping them both get their social security benefits situated, and doctor care set up to support their illnesses. Armina's memory and delusions were so much better now that she was on medication and didn't have to spend each day trying to survive the hunger and elements. The stress of her life in the city had made her condition so much worse.

Meanwhile, Lucy and Jorge were staying with Taylor and Sam, tucked into Lennon's room converted into a guest room. It was temporary, but it felt like a breath of fresh air. Like coming

EPILOGUE

home, again. Her big sister looking out for her daily as she had when they were kids.

Taylor stepped onto the porch with Lennon nestled against her shoulder, the baby's bare feet kicking at the warm summer air. Sam trailed behind, brushing sawdust from his jeans as he dropped onto the stoop beside her.

"How's the wiring coming along?" Lucy asked, sitting up straighter with a smile.

"Wrapped up this morning," Sam replied. "Floors are next. Having Jorge on the crew's been a game changer—things are moving faster."

"Aww, you tease," Jorge said. "I am a slow learner using my hands in this way."

Lucy couldn't help the warmth that bloomed in her chest. She loved watching Jorge out there with the others, sleeves rolled, jeans dusty, hammer in hand instead of a paintbrush. Sometimes lifting beams with his muscles rippling, laughing alongside Sam and Ellis as they taught him the ropes. Skills he'd take with him—gifts from her family.

"Quig's beside herself," Taylor added. "Keeps asking when she can start decorating."

Lucy laughed. "I still can't believe it. Her own cabin. Her own place."

"She's never had anything that was truly hers," Taylor said, rocking the baby gently. "Now she'll have a real home. And soon ... her kids."

"Cate offered her a full-time position at the boarding kennels," Jorge added. "She's a natural with the dogs."

"She's earned it," Taylor said. "I'm glad she's not going back to that old life."

There were conditions though. They would continue to monitor Quig with random drug-testing, and encourage meeting

EPILOGUE

her personal goals and attending an addiction support group, until they felt she was ready to be independent of their supervision. Taylor may have brought her into the fold, but Cate was championing Quig all the way, probably some of that because of their shared jail experiences.

Lucy leaned back, soaking it all in—the warmth, the quiet, the sound of a child cooing. A farm humming with new purpose.

"Speaking of jobs ..." Lucy looked at Taylor sideways. "When are you going back to the sheriff's office? Wasn't it supposed to be this week?"

Taylor and Sam exchanged a glance, and Taylor smiled.

"I'm not."

Lucy blinked. "What?"

"She's not going back. We've decided to open our own private investigation firm," Sam said, grinning.

"Missing persons. Cold cases," Taylor added. "Sam was amazing in Mexico. We made a hell of a team. We can pick and choose our cases this way, without sacrificing so much family time."

Lucy beamed. "That's incredible. What are you calling it?"

Taylor grinned. "Graystone Investigations."

Margot, still flipping pages behind them, called out, "Classy."

They all laughed. Now that she was off the streets, Margot was full of opinions on what was tasteful and what wasn't—things she'd learned from her own upscale life before her downfall.

"Papa, can we go see the new chickens?" Johnny asked, his blue eyes shining up at Jorge.

Lucy nearly melted. No one had told him to use that endearment. It had come out of her son's mouth the fourth night in a row that he'd insisted Jorge give him his bath, read his story,

EPILOGUE

and put him to bed. He and Jorge had connected instantly, as though they were always meant to be together as father and son.

"We sure can, buddy," Jorge said. He held a hand to Lucy, helping her up. "But not without your mama. She hasn't had her walk today."

"And Alice," Johnny insisted.

Arm in arm, they ambled up the dirt path toward the barn behind Johnny and Alice. The kids skipped ahead, Johnny launching into a story about monsters and chicken eggs that hatched with teeth.

Lucy smiled, her heart aching in the best way.

Johnny had grown in the time she'd been gone. His sentences were longer, his stories more vivid. But when she'd arrived and woken him up with kisses all over his face, he'd cried and wrapped his skinny arms around her neck. They'd wept together while she whispered to him over and over, "I'm never leaving you again."

She stumbled on a rock and Jorge caught her, stabilizing her. "I'm getting so clumsy."

"No, you're not. You just don't look where you are going." He laughed.

Alice was up ahead telling Johnny about school starting again. "I'll be gone in the daytime, but I'll be home after," she assured him.

Johnny pouted briefly. Then saw a chicken and took off running, shouting, "HENRIETTA!"

Behind the barn in the new chicken pen, Carmen's husband —Alejandro—stood beside Cecil, stacking hay bales. His T-shirt clung to his back in the heat, but he smiled easily.

"You're a hard worker," Lucy said as they passed. "Cecil speaks highly of you."

"He's good to me," Alejandro replied in his warm accent, giving Cecil a grateful smile. "And now Carmen can stay home.

EPILOGUE

She says she's in early retirement. Learning how to crochet and planning her own garden for next year. Very little housework from now on though."

"Don't forget," Cecil added, slapping Alejandro on the back. "She also said you're on your own when it comes to laundry."

They all laughed.

Lucy couldn't stop smiling.

The farm. Her people. Her peace.

She was beyond blessed that she would always have this, her sanctuary, whenever she needed it in life.

At the storage corner there was a pallet stacked high with dog food bags. On top, Lucy spotted a handwritten note in clean, looping script:

For the girl who saved my painting — and the animals that will save someone else. Love, Jackie.

Lucy smiled. Everything had worked out in Jackie's favor. She still had her painting, and, now that Ian's reputation was ruined, even in death, she held the top dog spot in the art arena for New York, though they both knew it wouldn't be for long. Jackie was tired of the competition and would be cashing in her chips and soon leaving for her own peaceful sanctuary, wherever it may be.

A rush of laughter sounded behind them and soon, Johnny had all his cousins with him, competing for which chicken to catch and hold. Bronwyn squealed while the rooster chased her onto a hay bale.

Lucy and Jorge leaned against the fence, watching the children. Ginger had followed and now lay in the shade with her tongue out, panting and happy. She thought of the other Ginger, and missed her sweet face, but it was worth the loss for her to stop by Oklahoma City and return her to Graham, along with an apology for leaving like she had.

EPILOGUE

He'd forgiven her quickly, glad that she was okay. He seemed relieved that she was no longer traveling aimlessly alone and had reunited with Jorge. He'd cooked for them, good ole smoked ribs, baked beans, and potato salad. The next morning, he sent the four of them off with a hearty breakfast and a promise that, if they ever needed him, they could call or show up on his doorstep, uninvited. Jorge had been amazed at this hospitality, and Lucy laughed, warning him that it was just a sliver of what he'd feel from strangers in Georgia.

Graham's feast was the celebration dinner after their day at the courthouse, pledging their love and commitment to each other, under God and Oklahoma law. With Graham and the Golden Girls as witnesses—all of them dressed in items they'd found at a vintage store in town after two hours of shopping and dress-up—they'd left the courthouse feeling triumphant.

Margot had even rallied. She'd found Lucy the perfect dress, a romantic vintage-inspired pale cream bias-cut slip dress, fine beads and sequins scattered throughout, sparkling under the sun as they made their way up the courthouse steps. It was delicate and beautiful, and Jorge had cried when he saw her walking out of the dressing room with it on.

At least the dress was traditional, as was his suit. Everything else was a rush of just-get-it-done so they could get back on the road. Yet still, it was a day full of laughter and impulsiveness, and she didn't regret a single minute of it.

Anna had given her a mouthful, though. When they'd arrived back to the farm and pulled the marriage certificate out, Lucy had introduced Jorge to everyone as her husband. Anna loved any kind of event planning, and she said she'd gotten shorted.

Jorge had soon charmed her, though, mollifying her into joining the rest of the family in congratulation wishes and hugs —after their shock, obviously.

EPILOGUE

Now her husband bumped her shoulder gently, bringing her back to the present. "There's an update you might want to hear," he said quietly.

Lucy sighed. "What now?"

"You ready?"

She nodded. She trusted him to deliver it gently. She was only getting news fed through him, just the facts and not the sensationalized versions that sent her anxiety into a flareup. She and Jorge were seeing her doctors together, as a team, and she was feeling mentally healthier than she ever had in her life. Medication and therapy were sending her demons away, and she no longer carried a blanket of paranoia around her shoulders.

"They're extraditing Suki's father. He'll stand trial in New York."

Lucy nodded slowly. "Good."

"And Suki ..." Jorge hesitated. "She's got a high-powered legal team too. Supposedly even better than her father's. They're going for accessory under duress. Experts are lining up to testify about the pressure she's been under for years. If they pull it off, she'll do some time ... but not much."

Lucy's jaw clenched. She didn't know what she felt. A twinge of guilt. A flicker of anger. And something else—maybe sadness. Suki hadn't led an easy life either, despite the glamour.

"She was a product of them," she said softly. "But she made her choices. Just like I did."

"You think you'll be called to testify?"

Lucy looked away toward the woods. "If they do, it'll have to be from five thousand miles away."

Jorge reached into his back pocket and handed her a folded envelope. "Amen to that. On that note, I got our tickets."

She unfolded it—first class. Three seats.

She looked up sharply. "First class? Really?"

EPILOGUE

Jorge smiled gently and rested a hand on her stomach. "Only the best for you and Johnny, *Cariño mío*. I cannot wait to paint you ... standing in the moonlight, belly draped in the most exquisite muslin dress, our child growing beneath."

A single tear slid down Lucy's cheek. She touched her stomach, barely rounded, already cherished. "I hope she has your eyes," she whispered. "And your quiet mind. No ghosts floating around in there."

He touched her cheek. "She'll have your strength. That's what is most important."

She turned toward him, arms wrapping around his neck. He smelled like cedar and salt now. His cotton shirt was soft at her cheek.

"Are you sure you're ready for this?" he asked.

Lucy pressed her lips to his ear, her voice steady and sure.

"Of course I'm ready. This is what I've been waiting for all my life. A true new beginning—with someone who knows all my flaws and still wants to be with me."

They stood like that in the golden light, with chickens squawking and kids laughing and dogs chasing butterflies.

It wasn't perfect.

No, it was better than perfect, and she couldn't wait to try to beat the same feeling in her new home, halfway across the world.

The End

A NOTE FROM THE AUTHOR

Hello, readers! I hope you enjoyed *Every Little Thing*, the twelfth book in the Hart's Ridge series. Thank you for riding along with me, Taylor, Lucy, and the gang! The true crime wrapped into the fictional town of Hart's Ridge and its fictional

EPILOGUE

characters was loosely inspired by a scary incident I read about in a Yelp review for one of Cabo's fanciest resorts.

If you've enjoyed this twelfth book of Hart's Ridge, I hope you will be kind enough to write a review on Amazon here. I would love to know if you're excited about this new direction for Taylor and Sam with Graystone Investigations! Send me an email at kay@kaybratt.com and tell me what you think about it! Your feedback is important to me. Book 13, NOW & THEN, and you can pre-order it now to hit your Kindle automatically!

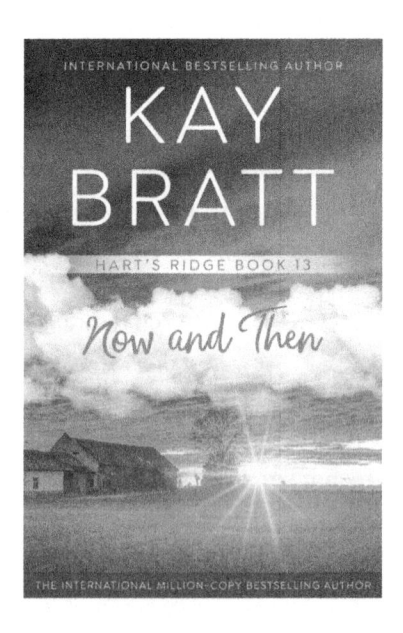

Now and Then

A woman sleuth. A cold case. A town full of secrets.

Taylor Gray has traded her badge for a new beginning. Alongside her husband Sam, she's launched Graystone Investigations—a private detective agency built on grit, intuition, and a

EPILOGUE

relentless pursuit of justice. It hasn't been easy, but now they've landed a high-stakes mystery that could change everything.

A man has spent nearly a decade behind bars for a brutal crime—but did he do it? Or was he a convenient suspect in a case the town wanted quickly closed? Hired by the man's sister to uncover the truth, Taylor dives headfirst into a tangled web of old grudges, missing evidence, and small-town whispers that don't quite add up.

With her sharp instincts and unshakable resolve, this determined women sleuth is about to uncover more than just the truth—she's about to stir up a past that many would rather forget.

From the bestselling author of *Hart's Ridge* comes a gripping new mystery full of heart, suspense, and the kind of justice only Taylor Gray can deliver.

If you'd like to be notified when there is a new title and pre-order button for another book in this series, you can sign up for my monthly newsletter at the following link:

JOIN KAY'S NEWSLETTER HERE

While you're waiting on your next Hart's Ridge book, I have many more titles for you to read! I'd love for you to check out my *By The Sea* trilogy, starting with True to Me: a mystery with lots of family drama with a twist readers don't see coming! Or if you love emotional family stories inspired by true events, you may like The Scavenger's Daughters series.

I'd also like to invite you to join my private Facebook group, Kay's Krew, where you can be part of my focus group, giving ideas for story details such as names, livelihoods, sneak peeks, etc. in my books. I'm also known to entertain with stories of my life with the Bratt Pack and all the kerfuffles I find myself

EPILOGUE

getting into. Please join my author newsletter to hear of future Hart's Ridge books, as well as giveaways and discounts.

Until then,

Scatter kindness everywhere.

Kay Bratt

Cover of True to Me. Woman walking alone on beach next to beautiful azure-colored water.

*Learn More about *True to Me* on Amazon at this link: My Book or keep scrolling to see the book description:

From the bestselling author of *Wish Me Home* comes a breathtaking novel about the secrets that families keep and one woman's illuminating search for the truth.

Quinn Maguire has a stable life, a fiancé and what she thinks is a clear vision for her future. All of that comes undone

EPILOGUE

by her mother's deathbed confession—the absentee father Quinn spent thirty years resenting is not her real father at all. With that one revealing whisper, Quinn embarks on a journey to Maui, her mother's childhood home, a storied paradise that holds the truth about her mother's past and all its secrets Quinn is determined to uncover.

But settling on the island has its complications, and, with the fiancé she left behind questioning every choice she makes, Quinn's quest for her truth is even more difficult than she expected. As time passes and she digs deeper into her family history and her own identity, one thing becomes clear: Maui is as beautiful as she'd always imagined, and its magic is helping uncover the woman that Quinn was always meant to be.

Get ***True to Me*** in eBook, Paperback, and Audio here:
My Book

EPILOGUE

Photo © 2021 Stephanie Crump Photography

Writer, Rescuer, Wanderer

Kay Bratt is the powerhouse author behind over 35 internationally bestselling books that span genres from mystery and women's fiction to memoir and historical fiction. Her books are renowned for delivering an emotional wallop wrapped in gripping storylines. Her Hart's Ridge small-town mystery series earned her the coveted title of Amazon All Star Author and continues to be one of her most successful projects out of her more than two million books sold around the world.

Kay's literary works have sparked lively book club discussions wide-reaching, with her works translated into multiple languages, including German, Korean, Chinese, Hungarian, Czech, and Estonian.

Beyond her writing, Kay passionately dedicates herself to rescue missions, championing animal welfare as the former Director of Advocacy for Yorkie Rescue of the Carolinas. She considers herself a lifelong advocate for children, having volunteered extensively in a Chinese orphanage and supported nonprofit organizations like An Orphan's Wish (AOW), Pearl River Outreach, and Love Without Boundaries. In the USA, Kay served as a Court Appointed Special Advocate (CASA) for abused and neglected children in Georgia, as well as spearheaded numerous outreach programs for underprivileged kids in South Carolina.

As a wanderlust-driven soul, Kay has called nearly three dozen different homes on two continents her own. Her globetrotting adventures have taken her to captivating destinations across Mexico, Thailand, Malaysia, China, the Philippines, Central America, the Bahamas, and Australia. Today, she and her soulmate of 30+ years find their sanctuary by the serene

EPILOGUE

banks of Lake Hartwell in Georgia, USA. Described as southern, spicy, and a touch sassy, Kay loves to share her life's antics with the Bratt Pack on social media. Follow her on Facebook, Twitter, and Instagram to join the fun and buckle up for the ride of a lifetime. Explore her popular catalog of published works at Kay Bratt Dot-Com and never miss a new release (or her latest Bratt Pack drama) by signing up for her monthly email newsletter. For more information, visit www.kaybratt.com.

Made in United States
North Haven, CT
15 September 2025